Warned

The Marquis awoke with a start and thought it must be morning.

Then he was aware that the room was in darkness except for the moonlight coming through the window.

Still half-asleep, he was aware that what had awoken him was a voice.

He saw to his astonishment that there was a woman standing by the fireplace.

"I am here to warn you," she was saying. "You are in danger . . . deadly danger . . . from a woman!"

Then, as the Marquis stared, she vanished . . .

A Camfield Novel of Love
by Barbara Cartland

"Barbara Cartland's novels are all distinguished by their intelligence, good sense, and good nature . . ."

—ROMANTIC TIMES

"Who could give better advice on how to keep your romance going strong than the world's most famous romance novelist, Barbara Cartland?"

—THE STAR

Camfield Place,
Hatfield
Hertfordshire,
England

Dearest Reader,

Camfield Novels of Love mark a very exciting era of my books with Jove. They have already published nearly two hundred of my titles since they became my first publisher in America, and now all my original paperback romances in the future will be published exclusively by them.

As you already know, Camfield Place in Hertfordshire is my home, which originally existed in 1275, but was rebuilt in 1867 by the grandfather of Beatrix Potter.

It was here in this lovely house, with the best view in the county, that she wrote *The Tale of Peter Rabbit*. Mr. McGregor's garden is exactly as she described it. The door in the wall that the fat little rabbit could not squeeze underneath and the goldfish pool where the white cat sat twitching its tail are still there.

I had Camfield Place blessed when I came here in 1950 and was so happy with my husband until he died, and now with my children and grandchildren, that I know the atmosphere is filled with love and we have all been very lucky.

It is easy here to write of love and I know you will enjoy the Camfield Novels of Love. Their plots are definitely exciting and the covers very romantic. They come to you, like all my books, with love.

Bless you,

CAMFIELD NOVELS OF LOVE
by Barbara Cartland

A NEW CAMFIELD NOVEL OF LOVE BY

BARBARA CARTLAND

Warned By a Ghost

JOVE BOOKS, NEW YORK

WARNED BY A GHOST

A Jove Book / published by arrangement with
the author

PRINTING HISTORY
Jove edition / October 1991

ISBN: 0-515-10692-5

Jove Books are published by The Berkley Publishing Group,
200 Madison Avenue, New York, New York 10016.
The name "JOVE" and the "J" logo
are trademarks belonging to Jove Publications, Inc.

PRINTED IN THE UNITED STATES OF AMERICA

10 9 8 7 6 5 4 3 2 1

Author's Note

IT is believed by some people who call themselves "psychic" that there are all kinds of ghosts.

The "Warning Ghosts," like the ones in this story, who appear to give notice of a forthcoming death or tragedy are different from the earthbound, unhappy spectres who are vengeful and send things flying around a room.

Or it can be love that binds them to this world after they have died, who haunt, carrying out the customs they observed in life.

For all of them a certain spiritual energy and awareness is necessary for them to "go on," but to do so needs a decision and independence of will that can take aeons of time to acquire.

During the First World War, I had lessons with a girl of my age, thirteen to sixteen, who lived in a lovely house in Somerset. It was, however, haunted.

There was always someone going upstairs in front of us and someone coming up behind. We used to hear a horse come up to the front-door, but when we looked out there was nothing there.

It was some years before I learned it was the home of a Royalist who had been wounded and who came home to die.

An Irishman told us there was a lovely woman with fair hair walking in the dining-room. We laughed at him, but five years later the workmen took up the huge flagstones in front of the fireplace.

Hidden was the body of a young woman with long, fair hair.

Even while they were looking at it, it disintegrated and fell into dust.

When I came to Camfield Place in 1950, I had the house Blessed, as I had no wish to live with ghosts.

It was after I had the house Blessed that I found in an autobiography of Beatrix Potter, whose grandfather altered the house and made it very much larger, that while she was here as a little girl she was frightened by ghosts in the hall and the large statues that were there.

There are, however, no ghosts there today, except for the ghost of a dog who was put to sleep after the Blessing and who has stayed with us because he loves us.

chapter one

1818

SEDELA rode across the Park looking for the deer underneath the oak trees.

In the distance on the other side of the lake she could see Windle Court.

It was a very fine example of the best architecture of the previous century.

She thought every time she saw it that it was even more beautiful than before.

There had always been a house there since the Windles had first come to the County in the reign of Henry VIII.

One generation after another had either pulled some of it down or added to the existing building until the 4th Marquis, sixty years ago, had altered the whole facade.

It was magnificent now with two wings stretching out from a centre building.

Although Sedela had known it since she was a small child, she always felt a little thrill when she looked at it.

She felt the same in the woods, the gardens,

and in the Greek Temple which stood at one end of the lake.

Sedela knew that the present Marquis had returned from France, and as she rode on she was thinking he would soon be coming home.

He was nine years older than she was. She had therefore only been a small girl when he had gone to war.

She had not often seen him before that because he was at School while she was still in the Nursery.

'I wonder if he will remember me?' she was thinking.

It would be strange if he did not, seeing that her father, General Sir Alexander Craven, and his father had been close friends.

When the late Marquis had died, the General had in fact been broken-hearted.

Sedela thought he missed more than anything else the games of Chess the two old gentlemen used to play in the afternoons.

Of course, they also discussed the war in its every aspect.

She often thought that her father had been as delighted as the Marquis when his son Ivan had won a medal for gallantry in Spain. Later he had also received the congratulations of the Duke of Wellington after the Battle of Waterloo.

"Thank God the war is over!" Sedela said fervently as she rode on.

She could not remember a time when England had not been battling against Napoleon.

Since peace had come three years ago, the country had been trying to recover prosperity.

She was aware that all Europe was trying to do the same thing.

'At least I can now persuade Papa to talk of something other than fighting and the horrors of war,' she thought.

Because he had no son, the General had given his only daughter what was really a boy's education.

She had not gone to School.

But he had engaged Tutors from the nearest Town and even from London to instruct her in the same subjects that he had studied when he was her age.

She had learnt to ride from the moment she could crawl.

She could shoot straight and she was exceptionally good at Archery.

She was reaching the end of the Park.

It had been dangerous to ride quickly because of rabbit-holes.

But now she was able to increase her pace.

She rode towards the front of the house, then turned right.

In a few seconds she came to the stables.

The cobbled yard had been washed down in the same manner as it had been when the old Marquis was alive.

The horses had their heads over the half-doors of their stalls.

She felt because she knew them all that they greeted her affectionately when they saw her.

A stable-lad came running to take hold of Fire-dragon's bridle.

"Marnin', Miss Sedela," he said.

"Good-morning, Sam," Sedela replied. "Is everything all right?"

"Foin, Miss Sedela," he answered. "We've two new 'orses 'roived yes'day from Lonnon."

"New horses?" Sedela exclaimed. "How exciting! I would like to see them, but first I must visit Nanny."

"Oi'll be a-waitin' to show 'em to ye, Miss Sedela."

Sam took Firedragon away to put him in a stall.

Sedela, now carrying the package she had held in front of her saddle, walked into the house through the back door.

She knew every inch of the long, flag-stoned passage.

She passed the Cool-Room, where the cream was forming on top of the milk. The huge open bowls stood on marble slabs.

After that, on the right, came the Servants' Hall, and on the left the huge kitchen.

From the high beams Sedela knew there would be hanging ducks, chickens, onions, hares, rabbits, and legs of pork.

She knew that Mrs. Benson, the Cook, who had been in the house for thirty years, would be delighted to see her.

But she walked on because her first visit must always be to Nanny.

Nanny was a very special person.

She was known to everybody in the house, on the Estate, and in the village.

They all spoke of her and addressed her as "Nanny."

Presumably she had another name, but it was doubtful if anybody knew it.

Nanny had been engaged twenty-seven years ago to look after the eagerly expected heir Master Ivan.

Son of the 5th Marquis of Windlesham, he was idolised from the moment he was born.

When Ivan had grown too old to need her services, Nanny had moved to General Sir Alexander Craven's house at the end of the village.

There she looked after Sedela.

She had stayed on at Four Gables until she found Sedela's Governesses intolerable and said she wished to retire.

"My son may be needing your services in a few years' time, Nanny," the Marquis of Windlesham had told her, "so you had better come back to Windle Court."

Nanny had been delighted to agree.

She found plenty with which to occupy herself at the Big House.

Besides, everybody in the village who needed advice or healing came to see her as a matter of course.

Nothing happened either big or small that Nanny did not know about.

Sedela knew that gossip flew from cottage to cottage as if it had wings.

But a good deal of it started from the Nurseries at Windle Court.

She passed the Pantry.

Hanson, the Butler, who had been at the Court for thirty-five years, had a new footman he was training.

Billy came from the village.

He was the son of the Estate Carpenter.

Sedela thought that when she came down-stairs again she would enquire how Billy was getting along.

She remembered her father saying he was a good lad.

It was traditional for the footmen at Windle Court to come from the village.

She climbed the stairs, and there were quite a lot of them, until she reached the Third Floor.

This was where the Nurseries were situated.

They were as impressive as the rest of the house.

The large Nursery looked East and caught the morning sun.

There were two bed-rooms, one of which Ivan had once occupied; the other was Nanny's.

There were two more rooms on the other side of the corridor.

These were for any child who might come to stay from time to time.

Sedela opened the Nursery door.

She found, as she expected, that Nanny was sitting by the fireside, crocheting.

Since she had no baby to look after, Nanny had added crocheted lace to practically every sheet in the house.

All the hand towels had six inches of crochet elegantly done at the hems.

Nanny was now starting on the pillow-cases.

She had grey hair and there were lines on her face that had not been there when she was young.

She still had, however, a warm friendliness in her eyes and the loving smile that Sedela had known as a child.

"Good-morning, Nanny!" she said. "I have brought you some of the cream cheese we have just made. Papa had a luncheon-party yesterday before leaving this morning with Mama. They are making a visit of a week or perhaps more to Mama's sister in Leicestershire, who is very ill. I know how much you enjoy this particular cheese."

"I need something to cheer me up," Nanny said in a low voice.

Sedela looked at her sharply.

"Cheer you up, Nanny? What is the matter?"

"I don't know how to tell you, Miss Sedela," Nanny answered. "I don't really! I can't bear that it should happen to him, of all people, my baby who I've never ceased to love."

Her voice broke on the last words, and she put a handkerchief up to her eyes.

Sedela went down on her knees beside her chair.

"What has happened, Nanny?" she asked. "What has upset you?"

"I knowed no good would come from him staying in London," Nanny said in a broken voice. "The things as goes on there are not for the likes of a man as brave and good as His Lordship."

Nanny had always been desperately afraid during the war that Ivan would be wounded or killed.

Sedela could hardly believe that once again she was listening to fear and unhappiness.

It was what had torn at all their hearts from the moment Ivan had left England to join his Regiment.

Sedela put out her hand to take the one in which Nanny was not holding her handkerchief.

Her fingers were stiff and cold.

"Tell me what has happened," she said soothingly, "and try not to cry, Nanny. You know how upsetting it is to everyone when you are in tears."

She had often thought that for a child to see her mother or her Nanny cry was something so upsetting that it was impossible to forget.

She could only once remember her own mother crying.

That was when her mother had died.

Nanny had cried when Ivan had got into trouble at School.

She had also wept bitterly when he had left to join Wellington's Army in Portugal.

"May God strike down that French devil!" Nanny had sobbed. "If he harms one hair of His Lordship's head, I will pray he'll burn in a Hell of his own making!"

Strong words, Sedela had thought, but Ivan had survived the war.

He had stayed, however, in France with the Duke of Wellington's Army of Occupation.

Then three months ago he had returned to England.

But to Nanny's consternation, he had not come home.

Everything had been made ready for him.

The House had been cleaned and polished

until, in the words of the General, it was "spick and span."

But His Lordship had stayed in London.

It seemed to Sedela extraordinary, but her father had understood that his services were required at the War Office.

"And, of course," the General said firmly, "the boy wants to make contact with his friends after being abroad for so many years."

Sedela told Nanny what her father had said.

She then guessed that Nanny, who was inclined to be a snob, was thinking the Marquis would be welcomed at Carlton House by the Prince Regent.

Perhaps His Royal Highness would want him to recount how he had won his medal for gallantry.

Anyway, Nanny would always make excuses for her "beloved baby," whatever he did.

It seemed incredible that now she should be in tears when he was back safely in England.

"What has happened?" Sedela asked again.

"I've had a letter from m' niece Lucy," Nanny replied.

She picked it up from where it lay on her lap.

She tried to read it, but the tears blinded her eyes and she gave it to Sedela.

"Read it for yourself," she said.

Sedela knew that Nanny's niece was Lady's-Maid to Lady Esther Hasting.

Lucy was the daughter of Nanny's elder sister and was now nearly forty.

She had been with various other Ladies of

Quality since she grew up.

Thinking quickly, Sedela remembered that Lady Esther Hasting was the daughter of a Duke.

She had married a soldier who had been killed at the Battle of Waterloo.

She opened the letter.

Having seen Lucy's hand-writing before, she knew it would be somewhat difficult to read.

Her spelling was extremely irregular.

Sedela read:

Dear Aunty Mary,

This is just a line to tell U that I'm very worried about the things as be goin on here.

As I tells U in me last letter, His Lordship's bin a reglar vistur an I hardly dares to tell U that Her Ladyship's made op her mind to marry him!

If he does anything so foolish all I can warn U is look oot for trouble cos there's no doubt U'll get it, an all them as is with U at the Big House.

Most of em 'll lose their jobs. Like I tells U afore no one stays with 'er Ladyship for more than a few months and there's em as says they'd sooner starve than work for her!

Hers only polite to me cause she wont easie find somun else as handy with a needle as I be which be thanks to U.

Her way with the rest of the staff is appallin n her screams at them like her were one o they rude women in Shepherd Market—but not to His Lordship—oh no! Nothin like that wen he's around. Sweet as honey, soft as a goose-filled matress an he ain't the least idea wot hers realy like.

*U'd hardly believe the men as sleeps here when
he's got other engagements and hers sure he
won't be coming here. Shockins wot I calls it!
There be one Lord Bayford as has somethin to
gain if Her Ladyship marrys as her intens His
Lordship.*

*I just happen to be passin the Bedroom late the
other night when they was conoddling each other
an I hears Lord B. say: "It wood be to my vantage
well as U Esther when U comes the Marchioness. U can count on me to get any obstables out
of the way, even if I has to shoot em!"*

*I'm tellin U this Aunty so's U'll be prepared
for the wors. But if her turns U out I knows there
be friends in the village as 'll find a place for U
somehow.*

> *Love to all,*
> *Lucy*

Sedela read the letter and felt it could not be
true.

How could Ivan, of all people, become involved with a woman who could deceive him
with other men and would be cruel to the old
servants like Nanny?

She folded the letter and put it in Nanny's lap.

"Perhaps Lucy is mistaken," she said slowly
after a moment.

"She's always been a truthful girl, Miss Sedela,"
Nanny replied. "She was brought up right by
me sister, and if she says that woman's bad,
she's bad!"

"But how can Ivan be so deceived by her?"
Sedela asked.

"Lucy told me in another letter that she's known as the most beautiful woman in England."

Sedela did not speak and Nanny went on:

"It's understandable for any young man who's been fighting for his country, then stuck in France with nothing but those Frenchies, who're not much to look at, to be deceived by a pretty face."

Nanny was championing her beloved Ivan again.

Sedela knew that nothing would be his fault.

At the same time, she was apprehensive.

Her father often said scathing things about the behaviour of those who belonged to the Social World.

He had been appalled by the extravagant parties which had been given in London by the Prince Regent, especially while the war was still on.

"Our men," he said angrily, "are fighting in the Peninsula to save England from the tyrant Bonaparte! Does no-one think of them?"

Sedela had heard the conversations that took place at home.

Her father's friends would come in for a drink after being out hunting. They spoke of the festivities in London.

She had also been present after she was sixteen at most of the dinner-parties given by her mother. Because she was there, the guests would choose their words with care.

But occasionally they forgot about her.

She learnt that the licence of what was called the *"Beau Ton"* horrified the country Dowagers.

Like Nanny, she could understand that Ivan, after the dangers and privations of war, would want to enjoy himself.

At the same time, it seemed heart-breaking that he should be caught up with a woman who could be as wicked as Lucy depicted her.

Sedela was sensible enough to know that servants exaggerated.

They also, like their "betters," enjoyed a tit-bit of gossip.

Yet she was quite certain that Lucy would not have written of such behaviour to Nanny, of all people, unless she believed that what she was saying was the truth.

It was also right for Nanny to know what to expect in the future.

"Could what Lucy feared really be possible?" Sedela asked herself.

Could Lady Esther Hasting really change the smooth-running, traditional manner in which everything at Windle Court was organised?

Every department was headed by servants who had been there for years.

They seemed to her to perform their duties with a perfection with which it would be difficult to find fault.

She knew only too well that if the older servants thought they were being taken to task unreasonably, there would be deep resentment.

The whole structure might collapse.

Her father and mother's household was conducted on a smaller scale in the same manner.

Sedela understood how the older servants thought of themselves as one of the family.

"We do this," and "We do that," they said to outsiders.

They identified themselves with their employers.

They spoke of Windle Court as "our house" because it was their home.

'Surely Ivan must be aware of this?' Sedela asked silently.

Nanny was still wiping her eyes, and Sedela said:

"If there is any question of your not being happy here, Nanny, you know your room is waiting for you at Four Gables."

She smiled and added: "I have always thought it unfair that Ivan should have you simply because he was born before me!"

Nanny gave a watery little laugh.

"I know there will be no question of my having to go to the Alms House," she said. "It's Master Ivan I'm worrying about. He was such a lovely baby, and many's the time he's put his arm round my neck after I've heard his prayers and said:

" 'I love you, Nanny! Promise you'll never leave me!' "

This story brought on another burst of tears.

Then Nanny blew her nose resolutely and said:

"There's nothing we can do about it, so we'll just have to wait and see, as the sayin' goes."

This was something Sedela had often heard Nanny say in the past.

"If only I could talk to Ivan," she replied rather helplessly. "Has no one heard when he is coming home?"

14

"He's coming back to-morrow for two nights," Nanny replied.

Sedela started.

"To-morrow? But nobody knows that!"

"I understand he told Mr. Mason he was not to tell anyone local. Master Ivan's coming only to attend the Hunt Meeting because he wants to take over the fox-hounds."

"Papa intends to go to that meeting," Sedela said, "but I am sure Sir Trevor Smithson will not wish to give up his position as Master."

"If His Lordship's made up his mind," Nanny replied, "it be a brave man who would oppose him!"

"So Ivan is coming here to-morrow night!" Sedela murmured.

"There won't be a chance of your seeing him, dearie," Nanny said. "He's arriving in time for a late dinner and made it quite clear he wishes to dine alone. He's going to the meeting in the morning, and trying out some new horses in the afternoon."

She paused before she went on:

"Then he's having dinner with the Lord Lieutenant and leaving for London after breakfast on Thursday."

Nanny paused because she was breathless, then added in a sad tone:

"I doubt, with all that planned, that I'll even set eyes on him!"

"It does seem unlikely," Sedela said, "and I suppose if I did say anything to him, he would not listen."

"Now, don't you go sticking your nose in

15

where it's not wanted!" Nanny said firmly. "You knows as well as I do I shouldn't be telling you these things, and Lucy would certainly get the sack if Her Ladyship was to know she'd written one word about it to anybody—let alone me— as is living in Windle Court."

Sedela knew this was true.

At the same time, every instinct in her body told her that she must do something.

If it was humanly possible, she must prevent Ivan from making a disastrous marriage.

She had not seen him for nearly eight years.

But everyone at Four Gables, from her father downwards, talked about him incessantly.

He had always been in her thoughts, and, in fact, a part of her life.

When she first heard he was coming home, she felt as excited about it as if he had been the brother she had never had.

"We are part of a family," she had told herself often.

In fact, her great-grandfather had married a Windle.

The old Marquis had shown her the name once on the long Family Tree which went back to the eleventh century.

'I have the same blood in my veins as Ivan,' she thought now, 'and somehow I have to save him!'

She knew, however, it would be a mistake to tell Nanny that.

Instead, she kissed her and said:

"All you have to do, Nanny, is to pray that somehow God will look after Ivan now as He did when he was fighting."

Her voice deepened as she went on:

"He has come home safely, and we cannot allow him to be hurt or injured by a woman who, from all Lucy says, is as dangerous as one of Bonaparte's cannons."

"You're right, Miss Sedela, that's the truth!" Nanny said. "And a dangerous woman can do more harm to a man than any bullet."

Sedela walked towards the door.

"Enjoy the cheese, Nanny," she said, "and do not keep it too long."

"I'll not do that," Nanny replied, "and thank you dearie, for thinking of me."

Sedela shut the Nursery door.

Once outside, she did not go downstairs immediately.

She was thinking.

"There must be something I can do," she told herself.

She walked to a window in the corridor and stood looking out over the garden.

The green lawn stretched away to a shrubbery of rhododendrons and lilac bushes.

Behind that there were young fir trees which had been planted on rising ground.

They formed a protection for the house against the North winds of Winter and the thunderstorms of Summer.

When Sedela looked at Windle Court from the other side, she saw it silhouetted against the green trees.

Sedela had often thought it was like a jewel in a velvet box.

Now she knew that nothing must spoil or destroy it.

There was something she had to prevent.

"He is in danger . . . please, God . . . Ivan is in danger," she prayed. "Save him . . . You must save him."

It was then, almost as if it were an answer from Heaven, she remembered Lady Constance.

Lady Constance had lived at the time of Cromwell.

She was the daughter of the 6th Earl of Windlesham.

Judging by her portrait that hung in the Picture Gallery, she was very beautiful.

She fell in love with a Royalist who had a price on his head.

He was being hunted by the Cromwellian troops.

He loved Lady Constance as much as she loved him.

He sent her a message saying he could no longer go on without seeing her.

He would come to Windle Court within the next three days.

No one ever knew whether he was betrayed by a servant, or it was just bad luck.

Lady Constance waited day and night, praying he would somehow reach her.

And yet the legend said she had a presentiment of disaster.

She was weeping long before news came that the man she loved had been captured.

The Cromwellian soldiers took him prisoner and hanged him on a gibbet.

It was a sad story which had been related to generation after generation of Windle children.

As the years passed, the family found that whenever there was danger or a death impending, Lady Constance would appear.

She would move through the house, crying and wringing her hands.

Each succeeding generation saw her before some disaster came—illness, death, sometimes a broken heart.

It was because there had been no sign of Lady Constance that Sedela had been sure Ivan would return safely from the war.

She had said this once to her father.

"You can hardly believe that 'Old Wives' Tale'!" the General growled.

"But I do believe it," Sedela insisted.

The old Marquis died while Ivan was fighting in Spain under Wellington.

Hanson, the Butler, Mrs. Benson, the Cook, and Nanny all swore they had seen the shadowy figure of Lady Constance moving through the Great Hall.

None of those people, Sedela knew, would have lied deliberately.

Now, as she thought of Lady Constance, she knew she had the answer as to how she could warn Ivan.

She could do it without his thinking that an outsider was interfering in his private life.

She was sure he would resent that. It would also be difficult for her to explain how, living in the depths of Hertfordshire, she could know what was going on in London.

Whatever happened, she must not involve Nanny.

'Lady Constance must tell him,' she thought, 'and I must somehow impersonate her.'

All those who had seen the ghost described her as thin from anxiety.

She also had long, fair hair that fell down to her waist.

Why her hair should be loose instead of neatly arranged had worried Sedela as a child.

Then she learnt that the news of her Royalist lover's death had come to her at night.

She must, therefore, Sedela reasoned, have run downstairs in her nightgown to see the messenger.

Her long hair had fallen over her shoulders.

At one time, because she was so interested in the story, she had read through the various reports of those who had seen Lady Constance.

They were all filed in the Library.

Some, which were written extremely badly with spelling even worse, were quite amusing.

"Her hair were a-shinin like a star," one woman wrote.

Another swore that her "feet did not touch the ground and she moved like a bird flighting over the lake."

"Her hair was glittering like a star!" Sedela said now.

Instead of going downstairs, she went up to a higher floor.

During the war these upper rooms had been closed.

The maid-servants who had slept in them previously were now in the top floor of the East Wing.

There were in the attics two large rooms.

As in all large houses, in them was stored everything that was no longer needed, but was too good to throw away.

There was Dresden china that was chipped, chairs with a leg or back broken.

But they were made of walnut or mahogany and had once been part of a set.

There were chests-of-drawers, and at the far end a number of wardrobes.

These contained clothes that had been used in the past for Nativity Plays given at Christmas time.

There were Fancy-Dresses for the parties which had taken place when Ivan was young.

It was to these wardrobes that Sedela made her way.

She was looking for something she could remember quite clearly.

She pulled open the drawers beneath the wardrobes.

After quite a long search she found what she was seeking.

It was a box that contained Sparkle.

She remembered Ivan's mother had sprinkled it on her hair when she had been the Fairy in a Play.

Nanny had had terrible trouble in brushing it out of her hair.

At the time she had looked very Fairylike in a dress that also glittered with tinsel.

She had a magic wand with a shining star at the end of it.

Sedela picked up the box.

Then she searched in the cupboard for what she vaguely remembered as a long piece of sparkling silver cloth.

It had been used on one occasion as a backdrop.

She found it and, carrying it under her arm, went downstairs.

At the far end of the First Floor there was the Master Suite.

It was where Ivan would sleep to-morrow night.

She guessed it had already been prepared for him and there would be no one about.

Swiftly she hurried down the passage.

Entering the bed-room, she saw, as she expected, that the windows were open and the bed made.

She knew the only thing lacking was flowers.

They would be brought in by the gardeners in the morning.

She crossed the room to the finely sculpted marble fireplace.

It faced the huge four-poster bed with its carved and gilded posts.

The Windle coat of arms stood on top of the canopy.

That, too, was carved and was not only gilded but also picked out in colour.

It was a room which Sedela had always felt should be used by a Knight in armour.

That, she thought, described Ivan.

Because it was a mistake to linger, she quickly felt along the panelling at the side of the fireplace.

The secret passages had been a joy to her ever since she was a child.

The late Marquis had allowed her to play in them whenever she wished.

They were, of course, only in the oldest part of the house.

The Architects of the last century had wisely left the old walls intact.

They had not bricked up the Priest's Hole which had been used when Queen Elizabeth persecuted the Catholics.

With the passages it had saved many lives.

But not the life of the lover of Lady Constance.

The secret panel swung open.

Sedela stepped into it and pulled it to behind her, then paused to adjust her eyes to the darkness.

There was just a faint glimmer of light to guide her.

She moved down the passage that was as familiar to her as those in her own home.

She reached the Priest's Hole and groped about for what she knew was there.

It was what she had always lit as a child.

It was a candle-lantern almost as old as the room itself.

It had a cross on the top of it.

The taper inside was half worn.

She lit it, thinking she must remember to bring another one to-morrow.

The light showed her the hard bed on which the Priest had slept.

On one wall was the altar at which he had prayed and given Communion to the Catholics in the house.

Sedela put down what she was carrying on a small table.

It would be waiting for her to-morrow night.

She blew out the candle and left.

She did not go back the way she had come.

Instead, she went down a farther passage to a lower floor.

She walked very carefully, aware that it would be easy to slip in the darkness.

She was familiar with every step and the walls on each side of her.

She therefore found her way without pausing to the Library on the Ground Floor.

She opened the door in the panelling.

She peeped through just in case somebody might be on the other side of it.

The Library was empty.

She stepped out from the fireplace and closed the panel behind her.

She listened to the tiny "click" as it went back into place.

There were few people left in the house who knew of the secret passages.

None of them would suspect her of using them.

Without hurrying, she walked from the Library and along the passage which led first to the Great Hall.

Then she went through to the kitchen-quarters

by which she had entered Windle Court.

She did not stop to talk to anybody.

She was only thinking as she went towards the stables of what Lady Constance must say to the Marquis of Windlesham.

She had to convince him that he was courting trouble.

Sam was waiting to show her proudly the new horses from London.

As Sedela rode home she was not thinking but praying.

She was praying with all her heart that she would be able to save Ivan.

chapter two

THE Marquis of Windlesham arrived home late.

It was nine o'clock before he brought his horses to a standstill outside the front-door.

Hanson greeted him respectfully, but with unconcealed pleasure.

As he drove over his own land the Marquis had been thinking that he had been very remiss in not having come home before.

He had, however, been in constant demand, by the Prime Minister, the War Office and, most persistent of all, the Prince Regent.

It was well known that His Royal Highness liked to know about everything that was happening abroad.

The Marquis had found himself spending hours at Carlton House just talking.

He was, in fact, most successful at entertaining the Prince Regent with his account of the Battle of Waterloo.

He also delighted His Royal Highness with the dramas which had occurred while the Army of Occupation was at Cambrai.

Because it was equivalent to a Royal Command, he felt obliged to attend the evening parties at Carlton House.

It was not surprising that he found relief and delight in the company of beautiful women.

The most beautiful was Lady Esther Hasting.

The Marquis would not have been human if, after the years of privation, he had not been entranced by her.

He also enjoyed the flattery received from every woman he met.

It was only one step further to find himself holding a soft, scented body in his arms.

The great Beauties of London looked what they were—"Blue-Blooded."

They had a dignity and a poise that was exceptional.

So he was somewhat surprised to find they were very different in bed.

Lady Esther was the most passionate, the most exotic, and certainly the most inflammatory woman he had ever met.

When he appeared in public with her, he knew that every man was envying him.

It was therefore extremely gratifying when she told him that she loved him.

"There has been no one, Ivan, in my life since Henry was killed," she said in a pathetic little voice, "and I have been very lonely."

She made it clear that she had spent most of the time she was in mourning in the country.

She had only recently come to London.

It goes without saying that she had been an immediate sensation.

Her beauty and her rank as the daughter of a Duke opened every door, including that of Carlton House.

It was not surprising that with so many people demanding his attention, the Marquis had hardly had a moment to think of himself.

Now, as he entered the house and saw the old servants he remembered as a boy, he knew he had come home.

It was home he had thought about as he had tossed and turned in some extremely uncomfortable lodging in Portugal.

It was home he dreamed about when he slept on the bare earth of Spain under a tattered tent.

It was home he longed for when, instead of returning to England after Waterloo, the Duke of Wellington had insisted that he go with him to Cambrai.

"I am very glad to be back, Hanson," he said as he took his Butler's hand.

He meant every word of it.

There was champagne waiting for him in a gold ice-cooler which bore his coat of arms.

Upstairs, the Valet who had looked after his father had a bath ready for him in the Master bed-room.

After it, the Marquis was helped into the evening clothes which he had worn before he had gone to the Peninsula.

Downstairs in the huge Dining-Room, which had remained unchanged since the Restoration, he ate an excellent dinner.

"Give Mrs. Benson my compliments," he said to Hanson as he finished, "and tell her I shall be coming home as soon as possible, if for nothing else, to enjoy her excellent food!"

"We've all been wanting Your Lordship back with us," Hanson replied.

"Thank you," the Marquis said as he smiled. "It is what I want myself, and it will not be long now before I am able to leave London."

"I thought that was what Your Lordship would be doing when two new horses arrived," Hanson said.

"I shall ride them to-morrow afternoon," the Marquis said, "but I have to leave very early on Thursday morning, as I have an appointment at the War Office."

"I understand, M'lord," Hanson answered, "and I knows how proud His Late Lordship, your father, would have been of you if he'd been alive."

The Marquis knew this was true.

As he left the Dining-Room he went into the Study, which had always been his father's favourite room.

He almost expected to find him sitting at his desk with a pile of papers in front of him.

He had always been very insistent on knowing everything that happened on the Estate.

Before anyone was paid, he inspected every bill.

"If you want a thing done properly, my boy, you must do it yourself," he had said a thousand times to his son.

The Marquis had found that was true on active service.

He had grumbled at the extra work it entailed.

Yet he knew that the success of his own troopers was entirely due to his meticulous organisation of their training.

He thought now there were an enormous number of things to be done on the Estate.

He already had new ideas for farming the land, for breeding his sheep and cows, and, of course, for training his horses.

He had often thought that in some ways Windle Court was behind the times.

While he appreciated tradition, he knew that innovation was essential for progress and prosperity.

One thing he had no wish to change, however, was the house itself.

He looked round his father's Study.

He appreciated the excellent picture by Stubbs over the mantelshelf and others by Aukin.

Horses painted by other artists decorated the walls.

The newspapers were laid out as they always had been on a stool in front of the fireplace.

He glanced at them but felt that he was too tired to read them.

It was hardly surprising, as he had not left Esther's bed until it was nearly dawn.

Even then she had protested.

"I shall miss you desperately for the next two nights," she said. "Oh, Ivan, why must you leave me?"

"I will be back on Thursday," he replied, "and we will dine together then."

She smiled at him before giving a little cry.

"Have you forgotten," she exclaimed, "that the

Devonshires have a dinner that evening to which we are both invited?"

"We will make an excuse not to go," the Marquis answered.

He thought she was going to agree.

Then she said in her soft, coaxing voice:

"You know, dearest, I would rather be alone with you than have dinner in Heaven! But the Duchess has been very kind to me, and is also already captivated by you."

She hesitated before she added:

"She said the last time I was with her that we were the most handsome couple in the whole country!"

The Marquis did not reply.

He knew exactly what Esther was insinuating.

She had, in fact, made it very clear to him in the last few days what she wanted.

It was not surprising, for women had wanted to marry him since he had left Eton.

He had had to extricate himself with difficulty from several "designing mamas" even before he left for Portugal aged only nineteen.

He had learnt during the years of war that it was dangerous to be impulsive, and sometimes disastrous.

Some cautious streak in him told him that Esther was "rushing her fences."

It was something he never did when he was on a horse.

To preclude a controversial conversation, he kissed her.

It was a gentle kiss, without the passion that had raged through them earlier in the evening.

"Good-night, my dearest," he said. "Take care of yourself, and if we have to go to the Devonshires on Thursday, we will leave early. Then you can tell me how much you have missed me."

"It will be agony without you!" Esther replied. "I love you, Ivan! I love you, and when you are not there, the whole world is dark and empty."

The Marquis kissed her hands one after the other.

Then, leaving the bed-room, he closed the door quietly behind him.

As he went downstairs, walking cautiously in the darkness, Lady Esther flung herself back against the pillows.

She had been certain after their love-making to-night that he would say the four words she wanted to hear.

Yet once again he had eluded her.

"I will make him say them!" she vowed. "I will make him!"

She snuggled down under the bed-clothes.

She was thinking of how fantastic she would look in the Windlesham tiara at the Opening of Parliament.

The Windlesham pearls would enhance the translucence of her white skin.

Walking back to Windle House in Grosvenor Square, the Marquis had enjoyed the freshness of the dawn air.

He was thinking of how the next morning he would wake up at home.

"I will ride before breakfast," he promised himself.

* * *

It was now he remembered that promise.

If he was to be called at six-thirty, as he intended, he had better go to bed.

The Marquis was very abstemious, owing to his determination to be fit and strong.

He therefore never suffered, as so many of his contemporaries did, from a hangover in the morning.

Yet even he found the rigours of the passion he encountered with Lady Esther fatiguing.

Her beauty was certainly exceptional, but so were her desires.

The Marquis could understand why these were so demanding.

As she had told him, she had been a year after her husband's death without the solace of love.

"Until I met you, darling, wonderful Ivan," she murmured, "no man attracted me, and of course living in the country or only staying with elderly relations when I was in London, I did not meet many."

"How can I be anything but thankful for that?" the Marquis had asked.

Then her arms were round his neck and her lips were on his.

Now, as he walked upstairs, he noted that the night-footman was already on duty in the hall.

He had said good-night to Hanson.

The Butler would not retire to his own quarters until he was sure there was nothing more His Lordship wanted before he went to bed.

"It is just as it used to be in the past," the Marquis told himself, "and I am very lucky to have servants like Hanson and Mrs. Benson who know exactly how Windle Court should be run."

Groves, the Valet, was waiting up for him.

"Now, you get a good sleep to-night, M'Lord," he said. "All them late nights I expects you have in London don't do nobody any good."

"You are right there, Groves," the Marquis answered in an amused voice, "and a good sleep is exactly what I intend to have."

He got into the huge bed which had been used by a long succession of his ancestors.

He appreciated the softness of the mattress.

The linen pillow-cases smelled of lavender.

It was his mother who had always insisted that the lavender-bags in the Linen Cupboard should be changed every year.

The Marchioness before her, and several Marchionesses before that, had insisted on the same thing.

Before he got into bed, the Marquis had pulled back the curtains so that he could see the stars.

It was something he had always done since he was a small boy.

His mother had told him that one of them held the Guardian Angel who watched over him.

"Which one, Mama?" he asked eagerly.

"That, darling, you will find out as you grow older," his mother replied. "You will feel your Guardian Angel is with you during the day, and know that at night he is in the sky shining down and protecting you."

The Marquis had insisted on having his curtains pulled back in the Nursery.

Later, in every room in which he slept he did the same thing.

He was thinking now that his Guardian Angel had worked very hard on his behalf while he had been serving in the Peninsula.

He could not remember how many times a French bullet had missed him by a hair's breadth.

He had escaped from being taken prisoner by a few minutes.

A mortar-bomb which had landed a few inches from him had failed to explode.

He had lived to come home.

He was sure that was due to his Guardian Angel, who had watched over him and was doing so now.

"Thank you!" he said drowsily as he closed his eyes and fell asleep.

* * *

The Marquis awoke with a start and thought it must be morning.

Then he was aware that the room was in darkness except for the moonlight coming through the window.

Still half-asleep, he was aware that what had awoken him was a voice.

"Hear me . . . listen to me!" someone was saying.

It was a woman speaking.

It flashed through his mind that it was Esther, but quickly was aware that it was not.

He opened his eyes wider.

He saw to his astonishment that there was a

woman standing by the fireplace.

Her hair was glittering as if it were covered with tiny stars.

"I am here to warn you," she was saying. "You are in danger . . . deadly danger . . . from a woman who is unfaithful to you with a man who is your enemy but to whom you have given your trust! Save yourself! Save yourself before it is too late . . . and remember . . . I have warned you of danger . . . danger . . . ."

Her voice died away.

Then, as the Marquis stared at the glitter of her hair, she vanished.

One moment she was there—the next she had gone.

The Marquis rubbed his eyes and sat up in bed.

He could hardly believe what he had heard and thought he must be dreaming.

Then he knew that the woman who had spoken to him was Lady Constance.

She was warning him, as she had warned the family for many generations when they were in danger.

"But Lady Constance has never been known to speak," he told himself.

He knew all the strange stories of her being seen weeping and wringing her hands when any member of the family was in danger.

He had heard about Lady Constance first as a small boy.

When he was older he read more about her in the records that were kept in the Library.

He had been on active service when his father died.

One of his relations had written to tell him that the servants had seen the ghost moving through the Great Hall before his father's death.

He remembered now that Mrs. Benson, Hanson, and Nanny had been positive that they had seen Lady Constance.

It did not surprise him.

He would have been surprised only if there had been no tales of Lady Constance.

Now Lady Constance had appeared in his bedroom to warn him of danger, then vanished.

Quite suddenly he knew how it had happened.

He got out of bed.

Walking to the secret panel at the side of the mantelpiece, he felt for the catch which opened it.

He did so in the dark, and he remembered exactly where it was.

As he pressed it, without a sound the panel opened.

He was certain that some woman had been impersonating Lady Constance, and he knew now how she had disappeared.

It took him a little time to put on his robe and light the candle beside his bed.

He carried it across the room and stepped through the open panel.

He remembered the secret passage and the steps which led downwards from his bedroom.

He had played in the passages after his father had shown them to him when he was about eight years old.

They had existed in this part of the house since it was first built.

He remembered jumping out at his friends when they came to stay.

He frightened the housemaids by appearing in a room they thought was empty.

He hid from his Tutors, and they had no idea where to look for him.

It had all been part of his childhood.

When he was older, he used the secret passages only when necessary.

He thought it important they should remain secret.

Now, as he walked along them, he told himself that some woman—and he could not think who—had had the impertinence to come to his bed-room.

Obviously she had thought it amusing to startle him with a lot of nonsense about his friends.

He reached the Priest's Room and, going in, found it empty.

He had half-expected to find the intruder hidden there.

But he saw the ancient candle-lantern on the table.

He touched it and found it was warm.

This confirmed that this was the way the woman pretending to be Lady Constance had reached his room.

Then he saw something sparkling on the wooden floor.

It was what she had worn on her hair which had given him the impression that it was covered with tiny stars.

"I must find out who this woman is!" he told himself angrily.

Carrying the candle, he went from the Priest's Room back into the passage.

He knew, however, that by this time she would have escaped.

There was little point in going down the passage any farther.

He knew there was a passage that led down to the Library.

Another ended near the Chapel.

A third led to the room where the Records were kept and was seldom used.

They were all in the old part of the house.

The intruder could have left by any of these exits.

As the Marquis returned to his bed-room, he was determined that to-morrow he would make a thorough search.

He would find out who besides himself knew the secret of the passages.

And who had had the audacity to approach him in such a manner.

'It is grossly impertinent, and I will not accept it!' he thought angrily as he got back into bed.

As he lay down, however, he began to think about what the woman had said.

There seemed no reason, if it was a friend, for her to have warned him pretending to be Lady Constance, and then to disappear.

He recalled the words she had uttered.

He realised, and he thought it was stupid of him not to have been aware of it before, that the pretended Lady Constance was warning him against Esther.

He could hardly believe it was true.

Yet there was no other interpretation of what she had said.

"But how the devil," he asked himself, "could anybody here know about Esther?"

People were talking in London—of course they were.

But he could hardly believe that anyone he knew in London would take the trouble to travel down to Windle Court and appear as the Family Ghost.

After all, he had been home only a few hours.

"It makes no sense!" he exclaimed.

If it was somebody in London, he reasoned, how would they know about the secret passages?

The servants in the house knew they existed, especially those who had been here since he was a small boy.

But he doubted if they knew how to work the catches.

They had been very skilfully made.

He was quite certain that his father had never let Groves know where the catches were.

"Then who does know besides me?" the Marquis pondered.

Suddenly, almost as if a voice were telling him the truth, he remembered Sedela.

She had been only ten years old when he had last seen her.

But he remembered how his father had allowed her to come to the house whenever she wanted to.

She rode his horses.

The old Marquis had treated her as if she were

a relation—as, in fact, she was in a somewhat distant manner.

"Sedela!"

She would be about the right height by now, he thought.

She would know exactly how Lady Constance had been described in the reports.

She would have known about her "shining hair."

"But why? Why should she warn me against Esther?" the Marquis asked himself.

Now he was back to his previous question.

How was it possible that anyone at Windle Court or at Four Gables could know anything about Lady Esther Hasting and himself.

Yet apparently Sedela knew enough to warn him that Lady Esther was deceiving him.

"That is a lie at any rate, a complete and absolute lie!" he said angrily.

But he was sure he was right in his supposition about Sedela.

'I cannot think what has been happening to the child since I have been away,' he thought, 'but what she needs is a good spanking!'

He thought it disgraceful that a girl of her age should listen to slanderous gossip, and act on it!

He would visit Sedela at Four Gables to-morrow.

He would confront her and tell her what he thought of her behaviour.

'As it was the middle of the night and I had been asleep, I suppose I might have been deceived,' he thought angrily. 'But, thank God, I am too clever to be taken in by such nonsense!'

He turned it over in his mind, then added:

'Lady Constance indeed! How dare she have the impertinence to dress up in such a manner and try to deceive me with her lying gossip?'

He wondered who could have told her such a load of rubbish.

'I will make her tell me who it was,' he thought, 'even if I have to shake it out of her!'

He shut his eyes and turned over in an effort to go back to sleep.

Instead, he could hear Sedela's voice saying:

"You are in danger—deadly danger—save yourself!"

'She must have "bats in her belfry!" ' the Marquis decided. 'Esther loves me and I am certain she is completely faithful.'

To suggest that she was seeing another lover at the same time was utter nonsense.

Sedela had also referred to a friend.

She must have meant Roger Bayford, but he trusted him implicitly.

They had been at Eton together.

When the Marquis had come back to London, it was Roger who had been more helpful than anybody else.

He had told him who was the best Tailor, where he could buy new horses, including the two that he was going to try out to-morrow.

Roger had done a lot of negotiating for him when he himself was too busy.

He was at this moment arranging for him to have a specially built travelling-chariot.

It was to be smarter and faster than anything else on the road at the moment.

"No! Bayford is a damned good friend!" the Marquis said to himself. "I will not hear one word against him!"

He tried to sleep, but instead, he tossed and turned.

He was seething with indignation against the slurs that Sedela had cast upon Esther and Roger.

"Roger has been a good friend to me!" the Marquis repeated a dozen times.

At last his anger began to subside.

Yet he was still asking how such incredible lies could have reached the ears of anyone as young and as well-brought-up as Sedela.

The Marquis was certain that the General, even if he had heard any such gossip, would not have imparted it to his daughter.

He was a disciplinarian like his own father.

They both believed, however, that children should be protected from anything ugly or unpleasant, especially a girl.

"I will quash these rumours once and for all," the Marquis decided when it was nearly dawn. "I will return to London, ask Esther to marry me, and bring her back here as my future wife!"

He thought that would solve the problem and silence the wagging tongues.

He would deal very severely with anyone who spoke a word against her in the future.

It was then, at last, that he fell asleep.

*   *   *

The Marquis had been involved in war long enough to be able to be instantly alert the moment he woke.

He did not look, nor did he particularly feel, as if he had not slept all night.

He rode across the fields on a horse that, he thought, had not been in the stables when he had last been at home eight years ago.

He had reached a decision which he was sure he would not regret.

He rode back to the stables, intending to breakfast early so as not to be late for the Hunt Meeting.

It was to take place at St. Albans.

He was no longer feeling depressed, nor did he feel angry.

"Everything will be 'plain sailing' from now on," he told himself, "and if Sedela has damaged Esther's reputation, I will immediately make reparation by announcing our engagement in *The Gazette*."

He ate his breakfast hurriedly.

Then he left in his father's ancient Phaeton which was waiting at the front of the house.

It was drawn by two good horses, but he had already decided to have some better ones.

He was looking forward to riding, immediately after luncheon, the two which Roger Bayford had bought on his behalf.

He was too experienced a horseman to hurry over the purchase of new animals.

He drove towards St. Albans, tooling his horses

45

with an expertise for which he was famous.

He had made an important decision.

He knew that in his safe at Windle Court there were some engagement rings.

They had been handed down through the family since the first Earl of Windlesham had received his title at the Battle of Agincourt.

The Marquis thought he would choose the most beautiful.

He would take it with him to London, and he knew how thrilled Esther would be.

"She wants to be my wife," he ruminated, "and because she is so beautiful, she naturally has enemies!"

It must be some unpleasant, spiteful woman who was saying these things about her. Alternatively it was a man she had rebuffed.

The Hunt Meeting was only partially satisfactory.

The present Master, Sir Trevor Smithson, had spent a great deal of money on improving the hounds during the war, and had no wish to relinquish the pack unconditionally.

He did agree, however, that it was the Marquis's hereditary right to share the position with him.

The Marquis accepted this with a good grace.

He was aware that Sir Trevor was getting on in years.

If he ran the pack as he wished to, Sir Trevor would undoubtedly soon find it too strenuous and too demanding.

In the meantime, he accepted a partnership and promised he would spend a considerable amount of money in further improving the hounds and the horses of the huntsmen.

Driving back to Windle Court, the Marquis was in a very good temper.

It was only as he neared his home that he remembered he had intended to call on Sedela.

He was, however, already late for luncheon.

The horses were waiting for him to come to the stables as soon as he had finished it.

It was then he had another idea.

"What I will do," he told himself, "is go back to London this afternoon, ask Esther to marry me, then make Sedela apologise profusely!"

He smiled before he added:

"There will, of course, be nothing else she can do."

After luncheon he told Hanson he had a note he wanted taken by a groom immediately to the Lord Lieutenant.

The Butler, knowing he was expected there for dinner, looked slightly surprised.

"I find I need to return to London sooner than I had intended," the Marquis explained. "I had forgotten, and it was careless of me, that I have a very important engagement in London this evening which I cannot avoid."

"So Your Lordship will be leaving this afternoon?" Hanson asked.

"Immediately after I have ridden the horses," the Marquis replied. "But I will be back again soon, Hanson. Perhaps next week-end."

The Butler smiled.

"That's very good news, M'Lord, very good news indeed. There's a great many people as wants to speak to Your Lordship, including the Farmers."

"And I want to talk to them," the Marquis answered. "I may be bringing some guests with me, but I will let you know as soon as possible how many."

"I'll see to it that everything's in order, M'Lord."

"Oh, and by the way, Hanson," the Marquis said, "give me the key to the safe. There is something I want from it before I go."

"Very good, M'Lord."

The Marquis hurried out of the Dining-Room and walked quickly round to the stables.

Once he saw the new horses, he told himself that Bayford had been right in persuading him to buy them.

They had been expensive, but they were exceptionally fine stallions with a touch of Arab blood in them.

"Them's the best 'orses, M'Lord, as we've ever 'ad in t'stables," the Head Groom enthused.

"They will not be the last!" The Marquis smiled. "I intend to have some very good hunters before the Autumn, and the sooner you increase your staff, the better!"

This was welcome news.

The Marquis rode the horses, one after the other, around the paddock.

One of them jumped extremely well and the other, after further training, would, he thought, do as well.

Then he went back to the house and quickly changed his clothes.

Time was passing, and he knew it would be getting late before he reached London.

He was, in fact, over-optimistic.

The traffic in the outskirts of the City was extra-ordinarily heavy.

It was impossible to move quickly.

He had to wait at a standstill at one spot for an infuriatingly long time before he discovered there had been an accident ahead.

It had taken place just where the houses began.

It was impossible therefore either to leave the main road or to approach the City from a different direction.

Two wagons filled with goods for Covent Garden Market had collided with one another.

The ground was strewn with vegetables and coops of hens and chickens.

The drivers of the wagons were having a fierce altercation.

The wheels of their vehicles were locked together in a manner which took an unconscionable amount of time to disentangle.

The traffic in both directions was completely blocked.

The Marquis had to leave his Phaeton and organise a number of men passing by who had nothing particular to do.

He made them help to clear the road.

It was, in fact, entirely due to him that the argument between the two drivers ceased.

They started to attend to their horses.

It took more than twenty men to lift one of the wagons off the road.

Only then were the waiting carriages, wagons, and Phaetons free to trickle through and continue to their destinations.

It was after ten o'clock when the Marquis reached Windle House in Grosvenor Square.

He was not only dusty and hungry.

He was also feeling somewhat irritable.

By the time he had changed, eaten a hastily prepared dinner, and enjoyed a glass of champagne, it was nearly midnight.

"I hopes Your Lordship has a good night," the Butler said as the Marquis left the Dining-Room.

The Marquis did not answer because he was, in fact, still considering what he should do.

Then he told himself that having come all this way, he should fulfil his intention of proposing to Esther that night.

If she was impatient to hear him ask her to be his wife, he was impatient now to do so.

In the pocket of his evening-jacket he had the ring.

He had chosen it from the safe before leaving Windle Court.

He had been right in thinking there was a good selection available.

There were, in fact, eight rings, all of which had been engagement-rings at one time or another.

Some of the earlier ones were rather heavy.

The one he liked the best had been worn by the Countess of Windle, who had been an outstanding Beauty at the Court of Charles II.

The Marquis remembered her story with satisfaction.

Despite the fact that she attracted the roving eye of the King, she had remained faithful to her husband.

She had refused to allow King Charles even to kiss her.

"I had no idea," the King was reported as saying, "that I would ever have a Puritan at Court!"

The Countess had laughed at him.

In the family archives there were letters telling her husband how much she loved him.

There were also poems which he had written to her beauty and to her heart.

"That is what I want," the Marquis told himself as he put the ring into his pocket.

He knew how beautiful it would look on Esther's long, white fingers.

He thought as soon as he had the time he would write a poem to her.

It was a warm evening.

Although the footman in the Hall offered the Marquis his cape, he rejected it.

He also refused his hat and cane and thought the man looked somewhat surprised.

Instead, he just walked out through the front-door and round the corner.

It was only a short distance to South Street, where Esther had a small house.

It was situated between two much larger ones.

The Marquis had laughed at the way it was squeezed in between them.

"I believe they protect me," she said softly, "and as I am so alone, I need protection."

The look she had given the Marquis told him only too clearly what she wanted him to reply.

Instead, he had just kissed her.

Now, he told himself, he would say the words she longed to hear and watch her beautiful eyes light up.

Her looks, in some ways, were a contrast to her character.

She looked, he thought, almost as if she were a cold woman.

He knew that it was her breeding and the way she had been brought up which made her behave with such calm dignity.

This was the impression she gave to those who met her casually.

But he knew now her passion and insatiable desires which had ignited a consuming fire within him.

There was a touch of red in her hair, a suspicion of green in her eyes.

But for him, and for him only, she was as wild as a tigress in the jungle.

It was a compliment no man who was a man could resist.

The Marquis had felt tired when he arrived so late in London.

Now he could think only of Esther's happiness when he gave her the engagement-ring.

He vowed he would be everything she required as a lover.

He knew that the front-door of the house in South Street would be locked and bolted.

There was in Esther's small household no footman on night-duty.

There was, however, a Mews at the back of the house in which there were a number of stables.

He had often thought that Esther was not as secure as he would like her to be.

Now he thought he would put his apprehensions to the test.

He would enter her bed-room from the Mews and kiss her into wakefulness.

Then he would put the ring on her finger.

He was sure that she would find it exciting and very romantic to be woken in such a manner.

In the Peninsula the Marquis had taught his men to climb what seemed almost impossible mountains and buildings.

They had also learnt to do so silently and stealthily.

This had enabled them on occasions to take the enemy by surprise.

Twice it had resulted in their capturing a French stronghold without a shot being fired.

The Marquis therefore looked at the back of Esther's house with an experienced eye.

He looked up at her bed-room window.

His first task was to get up onto the sloping roof of her stable.

It was unoccupied because he had put his horses at her disposal.

He was wearing shoes which enabled him to climb onto it without slipping.

There was an iron safety-ladder fixed to one side of the house.

It stretched from the top floor to the First Floor.

If there were a fire, this would enable the servants who slept in the attics to escape.

The Marquis then climbed up the fire-escape to the level of Esther's bed-room.

Below her windows there ran a narrow protruding ledge just wide enough to give him not much more than a toe-hold.

He edged his way carefully along the ledge, holding on to the side of the house.

He reached safely the first window, which was Esther's ward-robe room.

From there it was only a matter of a few feet to the next window.

He had already noted from the ground that it was open.

He at first thought there was no light behind the curtains.

Then he remembered that they were of a heavy material.

They would not only keep the light from showing through, they would also prevent anybody in the bed-room from hearing a slight noise if he made one.

The Marquis, however, reached the open window without making a sound either with his feet or his hands.

He knew his troopers would have been proud of him.

Then, as he put one leg very cautiously over the sill, he stiffened.

Somebody inside the room was speaking.

It was a man.

chapter three

"You are very alluring, Esther, as you well know," Lord Bayford was saying. "I cannot, therefore, understand why you have not yet brought Ivan to the point."

"He will ask me, of course he will ask me," Esther replied. "It is only a question of time."

"Time is one thing neither of us have," Lord Bayford replied. "The Duns are becoming impatient!"

Lady Esther gave a deep sigh.

"I hate to tell you how high my bills are!"

"I thought you made old Charlie pay them!"

"He paid for some," Lady Esther admitted, "but then Ivan came along and I had to send him away. Anyway, his wife was becoming suspicious."

"You have to make Ivan ask you to be his wife!" Lord Bayford said urgently. "I only wish to God that I could marry you myself!"

"Oh, darling," Lady Esther replied in her cooing voice, "you know how wonderful that would be, but you are not a Marquis, and you are not rich!"

"For God's sake, do not rub it in!" Lord Bayford begged. "In the meantime, you are driving me crazy, as you always do!"

There was a note of passion in his voice.

The Marquis, who had been listening from the window-sill, thought things had gone far enough.

He found it hard to believe what he had heard.

He had not moved and had scarcely breathed since hearing Roger Bayford's voice.

Now he put his other leg over the sill and stood up behind the curtains.

It had flashed through his mind that he should go away without letting them know they had been overheard.

Then he told himself it would be more embarrassing to explain later than to confront them now.

He put up his hands and pulled back the curtains.

As he had realised while he was listening, Esther had a small cupid candelabrum alight by her bedside.

It held three candles.

The light seeping through the muslin curtains which fell from the corolla was also very alluring.

A few seconds passed before either of the people locked together in the bed realised there was a third person in the room.

Then, as Lord Bayford raised his head, Lady Esther gave a scream.

It was then the Marquis said:

"Good-evening! I hope I do not intrude!"

He spoke in a controlled, icy tone.

It had made any of his troopers who appeared in front of him on a charge tremble at the knees.

"What the devil are you doing here?" Lord Bayford demanded.

"I came to have a private conversation with Esther," the Marquis answered, "and to ask her a question which I know she has been waiting to hear, but I realise now that will be unnecessary."

He walked across the room towards the door.

"Good-night!" he said sarcastically. "I hope you both enjoy yourselves!"

It was then, as he unlocked the door, that Esther found her voice.

"Ivan! Ivan!" she cried. "I can explain everything!"

The Marquis did not speak, but he looked at her.

She saw the contempt in his eyes before he went from the room.

He shut the door quietly behind him and walked down the stairs.

When he reached the hall he could still hear in the distance their two voices.

He knew they were exclaiming wildly at what had just occurred.

His lips were set in a hard line as he let himself out through the front-door.

He pulled it to behind him.

Then he walked slowly back to Grosvenor Square, feeling breathless, as if he had been running in a long race.

When he reached his own bed-room he undressed without ringing for his Valet.

Only then did he feel as if he had been hit on the head with a bludgeon.

He had believed Esther's protestations of love: he had trusted Bayford.

It seemed incredible they had both deceived him.

He had thought their affection for him was genuine.

Now he knew they had only desired his money.

He pulled back the curtains from his window and got into bed.

Then as he looked up at the sky he remembered last night.

Sedela, impersonating Lady Constance, had stars in her long hair.

"She warned me and I did not believe her! But she was right—absolutely and completely right!"

He felt as if the knowledge of it stabbed him and drew blood.

Then, as he began to breathe more easily, he remembered his mother.

She had been right in saying that his Guardian Angel was protecting him.

If he had put Esther in what had been his mother's place as the Marchioness of Windlesham and then discovered that she was nothing but a whore, the humiliation of it would have been unbearable.

He was also well aware who Charlie was, who had paid off some of Esther's debts.

He was a rich, dissolute Peer whose sole occupation was going from *Boudoir* to *Boudoir*.

The fact that he had a wife and several children did not perturb him in the least.

Nor did it prevent him from pursuing every new Beauty who appeared on the Social Scene.

"Charlie—Roger—and how many more!" the Marquis asked himself savagely.

It was infuriating to realise that like any greenhorn he had believed everything that Esther had said to him.

Her "lonely existence" in the country was only a tale, a lie to evoke his sympathy.

She had lied and lied and lied.

She had lied when she swore that no other man had ever touched her since Henry Hastings had been killed.

She had lied when she said she loved him.

He felt he wanted to stab not her, but himself, for being so gullible.

Then he remembered that he had been saved— saved not only by his Guardian Angel.

Sedela pretending to be Lady Constance had come to warn him that he was in danger.

The danger had been that he might have married Esther.

Too late he would have discovered her perfidy.

He wondered how many other people were aware of what she was really like.

Had they been laughing at him behind his back?

He could imagine nothing more humiliating than to have entered a room with Esther as his wife and to know by the look on several of his friends' faces that they had been her lovers.

How could he have been taken in so completely?

How could he have been such a fool as to believe he had been the only man in her life besides her husband?

The Marquis had always prided himself on his perception.

They had teased him about it in the Army.

They said that he knew whether a man was a rogue even before there was any evidence of it.

He had indeed always been aware when a man told him the truth or if he was lying to save his skin.

He had believed Esther—yes, he had believed her.

What was even more infuriating, he had believed Bayford.

It seemed incredible how easily they had been able to deceive him.

He wondered about the other men who had slept with Esther.

Bayford had tricked him into buying expensive horses, carriages, and Heaven knows what else.

He would have taken a large percentage of the sales for himself.

Now that he knew the truth, the Marquis could see it all happening.

He realised how obtuse and stupid he had been.

"I know you are busy, old boy," Bayford had said almost every day in the last few weeks, "so I will look for the horses you want, and, of course, you must have a decent Phaeton! Just leave everything to me. I will see you are not cheated."

"Not cheated!" the Marquis murmured angrily.

Bayford had cheated him in more ways than one.

It was not only that, but that he had been taken for a fool.

A number of people in the Social World must be aware of it.

The Social World was one thing, but his home was something quite different.

How was it possible that Sedela, who had come to him last night, knew of his infatuation with Esther?

How did she know, too, that Bayford was untrustworthy?

He could still hear her soft voice waking him.

He knew she had dressed up as Lady Constance, hoping he would believe the family ghost when he might not believe her.

She knew how to reach him through the secret passages.

She had disappeared in the same way as she had entered his bed-room.

His father and her father, the General, had been close friends.

Their friendship had been very important to them.

He could remember long ago, before he left School, asking his father why Sedela had been allowed to know the secret of the passages.

She had just jumped out at him when he was writing his "Holiday Task" in the Library.

It had made him start so that a blot of ink had fallen on his Essay.

"What do you think you are doing?" he had asked angrily.

"I have something exciting to show you," she replied, "and you have been working all the morning."

"I have to get this Essay done," he said, "so just leave me alone!"

"I said I have something to show you!"

"What is it?" he asked somewhat reluctantly.

"Swallow has had her foal!"

He remembered jumping to his feet with excitement.

"She has? What is it like?"

"The most beautiful foal you have ever seen and exactly like Swallow!"

He remembered how he had forgotten his Essay and everything else except his favourite mare.

He had run towards the stables, Sedela following him like a small dog.

But how was it possible that Sedela knew anything about him and Esther?

He had not thought about Sedela in a long time.

'I suppose she must be grown up by now,' he ruminated. 'At the same time, she had no right to creep in on me in the way she used to as a child to warn me of things she had no business knowing about!'

He began to wonder who else at Windle Court knew of his affair with Esther.

If it was not somebody in the house, it was

even worse to think they were talking about him in the village.

Of one thing he was determined to make certain: the gossip should go no further.

He could imagine nothing more humiliating than that the Farmers and his tenants should be laughing at him.

Or, for that matter, that the people in the County should learn that he had made a complete fool of himself.

His father had always been exceedingly proud of the Windle name, which was highly respected in Hertfordshire.

He had also been respected among his Peers in the House of Lords.

He had been a regular attendant until he grew too old and ill to make the journey to London.

"One day you will take my place, Ivan," he said to his son, "and I know you will bring distinction to the family, not only on the battlefields but also in Parliament."

It was what the Marquis intended to do.

Now that he had left the Army he had the time to attend to his Estate.

Later he would consider what part he could play in politics.

He knew from what the Prime Minister had said the last time they had met that he was likely to be offered a junior Ministry.

He was not quite certain if that was something he wanted so soon.

Yet he was well aware that it was a compliment.

There were so many things to do, and he felt he needed a wife to help him.

Now he was aware that if, as he had intended, he had married Esther, it would have been the most disastrous action of his whole life.

Sedela had saved him.

At the same time, it annoyed him to think that he had needed to be saved, and even more that it should have been by a girl who was little more than a child.

"I will see her to-morrow," he decided.

He already knew he could not stay in London.

He was certain that Esther and Bayford would try their utmost to see him.

They would have concocted some explanation of their behaviour.

Esther, with "crocodile tears" in her eyes, would ask his forgiveness.

She would doubtless think up some plausible excuse for what had happened, perhaps that she had drunk too much and Bayford had taken advantage of her!

The Marquis could think of a dozen lies she could tell, any means by which she could extricate herself from the predicament she was in and reinstate herself in his affections.

He was sure that she and Bayford were, at this very moment, fabricating some "cock and bull" story which they hoped he would believe.

"I will not see them!" the Marquis said determinedly.

It was impossible to sleep, but he dozed a little just before dawn.

He rang for his Valet soon after six o'clock.

He ordered his fastest travelling-carriage and a fresh team of horses to be ready in an hour.

He was hurrying over his breakfast, when his Secretary, Mr. Mason, came into the room.

"I have just heard, My Lord," he said, "that you are returning to the country. Surely you do not have to make the journey to-day, having only just arrived?"

"I am returning to the country, Mason, because I find there is a great deal to be done on the Estate," the Marquis explained. "Cancel all my engagements and make it clear to any enquirers that I have no idea when I shall be returning to London."

Mr. Mason looked aghast.

"But—has Your Lordship forgotten that His Royal Highness and the Prime Minis—"

The Marquis put up his hand.

"I said *all* my engagements, Mason, and I meant *all*! Make it clear that I have gone to the country on family business and that you have no notion of when I might return."

He rose from the table as he finished speaking.

He went from the room, leaving his Secretary staring after him in consternation.

* * *

The new team of horses he was driving carried the Marquis swiftly out of London.

He had to appreciate that they were exceptional, not only in appearance, but also in speed.

At the same time, it annoyed him to remember that they had been purchased on his behalf by Bayford.

They reached Windle Court in what was record time.

There was a look of surprise on Hanson's face as the Marquis ran up the steps and walked into the hall.

"Welcome back, M'lord!" he exclaimed. "We were not expecting Your Lordship back so soon, and I hopes nothing's amiss?"

The Marquis handed a footman his hat and his driving-gloves and walked towards the Study.

"I wish to see Johnson," he said, "and then I require a horse to ride."

"Very good, M'Lord."

Johnson, who was the Estate Manager, was produced rather quicker than the Marquis had anticipated.

After making arrangements to see two of his Farmers that afternoon, he went upstairs to change his clothes.

"It's nice to 'ave Your Lordship back!" Groves said with satisfaction. "It's 'ere you belongs, M'Lord, an' there's no place like 'ome."

The Marquis answered him in curt monosyllables.

But Groves had been at the Court enough years to think of himself as one of the family.

"Now, what you've got to do, Master Iv—I mean M'Lord," he said, "is to get t' know th' people as 'ave bin prayin' for you an' admirin' you all th' years you've bin away."

The Marquis muttered a reply and Groves went on:

"Them in th' village loves you as if you be their own son, and if there's one person as has been looking forward to your return more'n anybody else, it's Miss Sedela—Your

Lordship knows who I mean—th' General's daughter."

"I know who you mean," the Marquis said grimly. "But why should she be looking forward to my return and wishing to see me? She was little more than a child when I went to the Peninsula."

"Her came here every day to cheer up your father, His late Lordship, an' many's the time I've 'eard 'er say to him:

" 'Now don't you worry! Ivan'll be safe. I feel it in my heart, and there's been no sign of Lady Constance!' "

The Marquis was listening, although he pretended not to.

"An' many's the time when th' news from Portugal were bad," Groves went on, "I've seen her prayin' in th' Chapel. An' it were 'er as always put fresh flowers in front of Your Lordship's picture in th' Blue Salon."

The Marquis remembered that the Blue Salon had always been his mother's favourite room.

The picture to which Groves was referring had been painted when he was eight years old.

He was curious and had to ask:

"Does Miss Sedela still come here even though my father is dead?"

" 'Course her do, M'Lord! She comes to see Nanny, if no one else."

"Nanny!"

The Marquis realised he had been very remiss in not thinking of her before.

Of course Nanny was still living at Windle Court.

She would, he knew, be longing for him to visit her.

He adjusted his tie in the mirror.

Without saying anything more, he allowed Groves to help him into his whipcord riding-jacket.

Then he walked down the corridor and up the stairs which led to the Nurseries.

He was thinking that because Esther had monopolised his thoughts since his return to England, he had forgotten Nanny.

He reached the Third Floor and opened the Nursery door.

The sunshine was pouring in and shining on Nanny's grey head as she sat crocheting.

As he entered she gave a cry of delight.

"Master Ivan! I thought you'd gone back to London!"

"I have come back, Nanny, because I wanted to see you," the Marquis answered.

He crossed the room and bent to kiss her on the cheek.

"How are you, Nanny? Have they been looking after you while I have been away?"

"I'm happy now that you're home," Nanny said. "Let me look at you! I can see that you've grown older since you've been away, and you're very much a man!"

The Marquis laughed and sat down in the chair beside Nanny.

"I was one of the lucky ones," he said, "and I am sure it was because you were praying that I would return safely."

"Would I be doing anything else?" Nanny

asked. "And it was Miss Sedela who said there was nothing else we could do but pray."

"I hear Sedela has been coming to the house to see you. What is she up to these days?"

He was hoping that Nanny might give him some clue that would reveal to him how Sedela knew about Esther.

"She's grown up into a lovely girl," Nanny said. "And now that Your Lordship's back, I expect you'll be giving parties, and you may be quite sure everybody 'll want to come to them."

"Parties?" the Marquis repeated vaguely.

"Some of your old friends 'll never come back—them as lost their lives in the war," Nanny said. "But the others 'll remember you and of course want to see you again—besides all them on the estate and in the village."

"You make me afraid it will take me a lifetime to get round them all." The Marquis smiled.

Nanny hesitated.

"You might like to give a party like your mother used to do when she was alive."

" 'I get to see everybody at least once a year, Nanny,' she said to me once. 'That means we are free to enjoy in small doses those I really like.' "

The Marquis laughed.

"I will certainly think about it, Nanny."

"I see you're going riding," Nanny said, looking at his breeches. "Where are you off to?"

"I was thinking of calling on Sedela," the Marquis replied.

He was watching Nanny closely as he spoke.

He thought if she knew Sedela had come to his bed-room pretending to be Lady Constance, there would be some hint of it in her eyes.

Alternatively, a little hesitation before she replied would tell him she was aware of it.

He was using his perception as he watched her, but Nanny only smiled and said:

"Now, that's a good idea! If there's anyone as has really worried over Your Lordship, it's Miss Sedela. She kept your father's spirit up, though, and mine too."

She gave a sigh before she added:

"When I was most anxious about you, Miss Sedela would say:

" 'He's safe, Nanny. I know he's safe. Just keep praying and believe the best, not the worst. It is our good thoughts that will protect him.' "

The Marquis rose to his feet.

"As I am going to be here for a long time, Nanny, I will see a lot of you."

"I hopes so," Nanny smiled, "but when are you going to fill these Nurseries? I'm ready and waiting, but there's no sign of your producing a baby for me."

The Marquis stiffened.

"I am afraid, Nanny," he replied in a hard voice, "you are going to be disappointed, I have no intention of marrying anyone."

He walked from the room as he spoke.

Nanny looked after him with a worried expression in her eyes.

'Now, who's been upsetting him, I'd like to know?' she reflected. 'If it's that woman in London, I'd like to wring her neck!'

The Marquis found that waiting at the front-
door was one of the new horses he had ridden
yesterday.

He was a stallion called Flash, a name the
Marquis thought very appropriate.

He swung himself into the saddle and he knew
he was going to enjoy the ride, if nothing else.

He set off at a sharp pace.

As he entered the Park he slowed down until
he reached the gate at the far end.

It was only a short distance from there to Four
Gables.

When he saw the house with its ancient red
bricks now faded to pink, he thought it looked
even more attractive than he remembered.

As a boy, he had always been slightly in awe
of the General.

Lady Craven, however, had been kind and
sweet to him.

He was remembering how beautiful she was.

"I wonder if Sedela resembles her?" he questioned.

Then he reminded himself of the reason for
his visit.

The resentment he had repressed up until now
began to rise within him.

How dare Sedela come to him pretending to
be Lady Constance?

If it came to that, how dare she meddle in his
private affairs?

Yet in the long run he had to admit that it had
been to his advantage.

As he dismounted, a groom came running from the stable to take Flash from him.

" 'Marnin', M'Lord!" he grinned. "That be a roight foin 'orse ye be a-ridin'!"

"That is what I was thinking as I came here," the Marquis replied.

He walked up the steps to the front-door and raised the knocker.

Even as he touched it the door opened and Sedela stood there.

"I saw you! I saw you from the window!" she exclaimed. "Oh, Ivan, you are back! I thought you had gone to London!"

"I have come to see you, Sedela," the Marquis replied.

He walked into the hall and put his hat and riding-gloves on a chair.

He was thinking as he did so that Sedela looked very different from how he remembered her.

She was lovely, lovely in a way he had not expected.

At the same time, she did not seem at all embarrassed at seeing him, which he thought strange.

Surely she was perturbed in case he should be aware it was she who had appeared as the Ghost?

Surely she must know it was reprehensible of her.

She should be feeling shy in case he guessed at the identity of his midnight visitor.

He followed her into the Drawing-Room which he remembered.

It had always looked very attractive with

its diamond-paned windows, low ceiling, and Queen Anne panelling painted white.

Every corner of the room appeared to be filled with fresh flowers.

They scented the air with their fragrance.

Automatically the Marquis walked towards the fireplace to stand with his back to it.

"I can hardly believe it is you!" Sedela said. "And looking just the same as you were before you went away, except perhaps that you are older."

"That is what Nanny said," the Marquis replied.

Sedela's face seemed to light up.

"You went up to see Nanny? I am so glad! She has been desperately worried about you all the time you were away at the war, and I was afraid you might forget to visit her."

"I hope I should not forget anyone as important as Nanny!" the Marquis said somewhat pompously.

He knew he was being a hypocrite.

At the same time, he was wondering how he could approach the purpose of his coming.

"I want to talk to you, Sedela," he said at length, "because the night before last a very strange thing happened."

He thought Sedela looked at him curiously.

Then, in a very quiet voice, he said slowly:

"Lady Constance came to warn me!"

"Lady Constance?" Sedela questioned.

He could hardly believe it, but she seemed perfectly at ease.

There was just the right intonation in her voice as she said the words.

"Lady Constance came to warn me," the Marquis repeated, "that I was in danger. The extraordinary thing is that she has never been known to speak before!"

Now he thought there was a flicker in Sedela's eyes.

She turned her face away as she sat down on a chair.

There was silence until she asked:

"Was it because of Lady Constance's warning that you returned home to-day, which I believe was quite unexpected?"

"I came back to ask you how you knew I was in danger!"

The colour came flooding into her cheeks.

There was a silence during which it she could hardly breathe.

Then she said in a very small voice:

"H-how did you . . . know it was . . . me?"

"I could think of no one else who knew of the secret," the Marquis replied, "and who had long, fair hair, as Lady Constance was supposed to have!"

He glanced at Sedela's hair as he spoke, which was neatly arranged at the back of her head.

He knew when it was loose it would fall over her shoulders and neatly to her waist.

Sedela rose to her feet.

"I . . . I am sorry if it . . . upset you," she said softly, "but . . . I could not think of . . . any other way of warning you."

She walked across the room as she spoke.

She stood at the window, looking out at the sundial in the centre of the rose-garden.

She had her back to the Marquis, and the sunshine turned her hair to gold.

After a moment he walked across the room to stand beside her.

"I want to know the truth, Sedela," he said. "Who told you about it?"

Sedela did not answer, and he said sternly:

"I intend to know who your informant was, and also who else here in the Country is aware of what has happening while I have been in London!

"I . . . I can answer your . . . last question," Sedela said. "There is only one other person here apart from myself who knows about your situation in London. Because I was . . . frightened of . . . what you . . . might do . . . I had to . . . find a way . . . of . . . warning you!"

"I still cannot understand who would talk to you, of all people, about such matters!" the Marquis said.

Sedela looked alarmed and, as he thought to himself innocent and untouched.

Suddenly it infuriated him to think she knew what sort of woman Esther Hasting was.

Because he felt so angry, he spoke more sharply than he otherwise might have done.

"Now, come along," he said, "do not lie to me! Who told you what I am sure is a quite exaggerated tale about me, and why did you take it upon yourself to interfere in my private life?"

His voice seemed to ring out harshly.

Then, as Sedela did not move or reply, he said:

"I think I'm entitled to know what you feared."

There was silence, until in a very small voice he could hardly hear, Sedela said:

"I was . . . afraid you . . . might m-marry somebody . . . who would . . . spoil . . . Windle Court and . . . and those . . . belonging to you . . . and who are . . . part of you."

The Marquis stared at Sedela's face.

How was it possible, he asked himself, that she could have the slightest idea he was considering marrying Esther?

Suddenly he put out his arms and took her by the shoulders.

"Look at me, Sedela!" he commanded. "I want you to tell me who has been talking to you, but, before you do so, I can assure you I have no intention whatever of marrying anybody. Let us get that quite clear from the beginning!"

Sedela gave an exclamation that was almost a cry.

Her eyes lit up and she asked:

"Is that true . . . really true? Oh, Ivan, I am glad! I have been so . . . worried about you! You know how . . . everybody . . . loved your mother . . . and how much she . . . meant to all who knew her. How could you . . . put somebody . . . wrong . . . in her place?

"I will put nobody in her place who is not worthy to be there," the Marquis replied. "But I still wish to know who told you I was contemplating anything that might hurt my home, or those—and I presume you mean my servants—who live in it!"

Sedela looked up at him, and he thought her eyes were shining like stars.

"Now that you have told me you are out of danger, there is no need for us to think about it any more," she said firmly. "Oh, Ivan, let us just be glad you are home, and there are so many people longing to see you and tell you how proud they are of your bravery! Papa and Mama would be the first to want to see you, but they have gone away on a visit to see Mama's sister, who is very ill."

chapter four

FOR a moment the Marquis thought of replying angrily that he wanted the truth.

Then, because Sedela looked so pretty and was so excited, he found himself saying:

"All right, we will forget all the trouble and decide what is important for me to do now."

"Do you mean that?" Sedela asked. "And . . . dare I tell . . . you . . . ?"

"I think you have dared quite enough already not to be afraid of over-stepping the mark further," he said a little sarcastically.

"Then what you have to do," Sedela said, "is to meet all the people who have been anxious about you and are so delighted now that you have come home."

"I seem to have heard this before," the Marquis said.

He was thinking of what Groves had said when he had helped him dress.

"I suppose from Nanny," Sedela suggested.

"Nanny and Groves," the Marquis answered.

"And I am sure Mrs. Benson and Hanson will say the same as soon as they get the chance," he added with mock resignation.

Sedela laughed.

"Then there is nothing you can do but capitulate and do what we all want."

"Well, what is it you want?" the Marquis asked, knowing the answer.

"I have just told you—that you have to meet everybody who thinks you are wonderful—and the easiest way to do that is to give a huge party."

The Marquis groaned.

"That is exactly what Nanny said, but it is something I have no wish to do."

"But you must," Sedela insisted, "because otherwise the people you visit first will be 'cock-a-hoop,' while everyone else who comes later will feel affronted."

The Marquis thought that in fact this was quite logical.

He wondered if he had made a mistake in visiting two Farmers this afternoon, unless he could see a number more very quickly.

He was aware that Sedela was watching his face anxiously.

After a moment he said:

"Very well—it shall be a party. But I cannot quite see how we combine the Lord Lieutenant and all the County 'Big-Wigs' with the villagers."

"That is quite easy," Sedela assured him, "and actually I have thought it out already."

"I might have guessed that," the Marquis said.

He walked to an armchair and sat down, crossing his legs.

"I am listening," he said. "At the same time, I shall resist you if you go too far or expect too much."

"What I thought," Sedela began, "is that you should invite everybody whom your mother used to have to her garden-parties, which, of course, means all the 'Big-Wigs.'"

"I am sure there are hundreds of those!" the Marquis remarked gloomily.

"Not as many as there were before the war," Sedela said quietly.

"And what next?" the Marquis enquired.

She hesitated a moment before she answered.

"When your father was alive and I was quite young, he promised me that one day he would have . . . a Circus in the . . . grounds."

The Marquis stared at her.

"A Circus?" he exclaimed.

"I think everyone would enjoy it," Sedela said. "Anyway, if the older people prefer to sit in the garden, their children will be thrilled at what happens in the Big Top."

She waited, and when he did not speak, she said pleadingly:

"Oh . . . please . . . let us have . . . a Circus! It is what I have . . . always wanted . . . myself. And, of course . . . fireworks!"

The Marquis looked startled, but suddenly he laughed.

"I do not know what I am letting myself in for," he said, "but I see your reasoning, and while we are doing it, we might as well do it properly."

Sedela clapped her hands.

"I thought, Ivan, you would be as eager as I am to start something new. You know a garden-party with people just sitting about is boring, and it would be a mistake on your part to entertain just your friends and not the people who work for you."

"All right," the Marquis said, "I agree to everything. You arrange it, and I will pay for it."

Sedela looked astonished.

"Do you really . . . mean for . . . me to . . . arrange . . . it?"

"Of course I do," he answered. "It was your idea, and you will have to do all the hard work. Anyway, as you are well aware, having been abroad for so long, I would be certain to leave out someone of importance who would then take umbrage and be a bitter enemy for the rest of my life!"

He was talking lightly, but Sedela took him seriously.

"That . . . unfortunately . . . is true," she said, "and I will be very . . . very careful that no one is . . . omitted."

The Marquis rose to his feet.

"Now, having settled that problem," he said, "I must go riding."

As he spoke, he saw the expression in Sedela's eyes and added:

"I suppose you want to come with me?"

"Just as I used to do," Sedela said. "Oh, Ivan, while you were away I have often thought of our rides, and rode alone in the woods and over the fields, where I used to try and race you."

She smiled before she finished.

"And you always . . . beat me . . . then."

"Are you suggesting that it might be different now that you are grown up?"

"Only if I had the right horse," Sedela retorted. "Papa has not bought any recently and, as you will find, some of the horses in your own stables are getting very old."

"I had two new ones to ride yesterday," the Marquis said.

"I know that," Sedela answered. "I have seen them and they are superb!"

"I rode over on Flash," the Marquis said, "and I will tell you what we will do."

He could see that Sedela was listening excitedly as he went on:

"We will go home and I will ride the other horse which I think needs a little more training, especially at the jumps, and you can ride Flash."

Sedela gave a cry of excitement and flung her arms round him.

"Thank you, thank you!" she cried.

She was hugging him impulsively, just as she used to do when she was a little girl.

Then, before he could put his arms round her, she was running across the room towards the door.

"I will change in two minutes," she said.

"Shall I order one of your own horses?" the Marquis called after her.

"I will ride pillion back to the Court," Sedela shouted back.

She disappeared, and the Marquis laughed.

She might be grown-up, but she was behaving just as she had when he had last seen her.

'I suppose I ought really to be angry with her,' he thought, 'but what is the point? And the less I think about Esther, the better!'

But because he *was* thinking of her, he felt a bitterness and anger creeping over him again.

With an effort he forced himself to take an interest in the garden.

He could see through the window it was well kept and just as attractive as he remembered it.

Then he walked into the room where the General had always sat.

There was a portrait of him over the mantelpiece, wearing his uniform, his medals pinned to his chest.

He had been a very handsome man in his youth.

He was dignified and somewhat awe-inspiring in his later years, when the portrait had been painted.

There were pictures on the wall of the places where he had been with his Regiment, and a few amusing cartoons which had been drawn of his brother officers and himself.

In the Chippendale bookcase there was, the Marquis knew, a great number of books on war and Biographies of famous Generals.

He heard Sedela calling for him, and he went from the Study to the hall.

She had changed into a riding-skirt and short boots.

Because it was hot, she was wearing with it only a white muslin blouse and no jacket.

"I am ready," she said, "and you must admit I have not kept you waiting long!"

"I am, of course, grateful," the Marquis said. "At the same time, do you really intend to ride behind me?"

"It is only just across the Park," Sedela replied, "and it seems a waste of time to saddle one of my horses."

She lowered her voice as if she felt she would be overheard before she added:

"Poor old Abbey is getting very old and very slow."

"I remember him," the Marquis said. "Do you mean to say he is still working for you?"

"It would break his heart if we put him . . . out to grass." Sedela smiled.

They went out through the front-door.

The boy who had taken Flash away when the Marquis arrived came hurrying with him from the stables.

"Have you had any trouble with him?" the Marquis asked.

"Nay, M'Lord, 'e's bin good as gold!" the lad replied.

The Marquis picked Sedela up in his arms and lifted her onto the saddle.

"I said I would sit behind you," she protested.

"Nonsense!" he replied. "We will ride as I used to see you riding with your father when you had just cut your first tooth."

Sedela laughed.

"All right," she said, "if you want to be uncomfortable, you go ahead. I expect whatever I say you will have your own way."

"Of course!" the Marquis declared. "You had better get used, now that I am home, to my giving you orders."

"Now you are definitely being pompous," Sedela objected, "and that is something you never used to be."

The Marquis had swung himself up onto the horse's back behind her.

Because she was so small and slender, there was room for him to sit on the back of the saddle and hold her in front of him.

He did not intend to go very fast.

As they moved into the Park he thought how lovely the sunshine was, coming through the trees and sparkling on Sedela's hair.

It made him think of how at first he had thought it was the stars on Lady Constance's.

He wanted once again to ask her who had told her about Lady Esther and Lord Bayford.

Then he knew that Sedela was right.

She had said it was a mistake now to think of anything except the present.

It took them only a short time to reach the stables.

The grooms looked surprised when they saw Sedela sitting on the front of the Marquis's saddle.

She slipped easily to the ground without any help and the Marquis dismounted.

"Saddle Mayflower," he ordered, "and Miss Sedela will ride Flash.

The grooms hurried to obey him, and Sedela asked:

"Are you going to buy any more horses?"

"I fully intend to," the Marquis said.

"Then there are some coming up for sale which I think you should look at."

"In Hertfordshire?" he asked.

She nodded.

"I do not think you will remember him, but there was a man, a newcomer to the County, called Reid, who bought Ashton House after Lord Ashton died, and had some very fine horses."

The Marquis was listening with interest as Sedela went on:

"Mr. Reid was an elderly man when he came here, and he intended setting up a stable for his son who, like you, was fighting Napoleon."

Before she said it, the Marquis knew the end of the story.

"And I suppose his son was killed!" he said.

Sedela nodded.

"It so shocked Mr. Reid that he had a heart-attack, and although he recovered partially, he died a few weeks ago."

"A sad story," the Marquis remarked quietly.

"There is to be a sale arranged by his Executors in a week's time," Sedela said. "I am sure it would be worth your while inspecting the horses now, before it takes place."

"We will go there immediately after luncheon," the Marquis said. "Now we will take Flash and Mayflower over the jumps."

He knew that Sedela was thrilled by the idea.

As soon as Mayflower was saddled, they entered the paddock.

Although the Marquis had a little trouble with

Mayflower, both horses appeared to enjoy the exercise.

Back at the house, Hanson told them that luncheon was ready.

"I will just wash my hands," Sedela said, running up the stairs.

The Marquis waited until she returned.

Mrs. Benson had prepared an excellent meal.

There were, however, so many things that Sedela wanted to tell the Marquis that he hardly knew what he was eating.

She gave him a summary of everything that had happened in the neighbourhood while he had been away.

She continually reiterated what a difference it would make now that he was home.

"There are so many things for you to do," she said, "but I was afraid that London would swallow you up."

"That is what it was trying to do," the Marquis admitted, "but I suppose my first duty is here."

"You know it is," Sedela said. "This is your kingdom, where you reign like a King. However important you may be in London, it cannot be the same as this."

"I doubt if many people would agree with you," the Marquis replied.

He saw Sedela's eyes flash before she asked:

"What do you really feel about it, Ivan?"

"You are trying to make me admit that you are right," he answered, "but I have to be convinced that being just a 'Country Squire' will not very quickly become nothing but a bore."

He was teasing Sedela, but she said angrily:

"How can you say anything so ridiculous? The Marquis of Windlesham could never be *just* a Country Squire, and the Farmers, not only in this County but everywhere in England, need somebody to champion them, now that they are being so badly treated."

The Marquis raised his eye-brows as she went on:

"You must be aware, even though you have been away, that prices for farm-produce have slumped now that the war is over, and Farmers are going bankrupt one after the other because they cannot sell their crops."

The Marquis knew this was true, but it had not occurred to him that it was something which called for action by him.

"If you want me to fight for the Farmers," he said, "I shall have to go to London to speak in the House of Lords."

"Of course you must do that," Sedela agreed, "but speaking in Parliament on behalf of the people is very different from—"

She stopped.

She was thinking of Lady Esther, and the Marquis knew what she was going to say.

Because he had no wish to discuss that subject with Sedela, he said:

"I think if we are going to Ashton House, we should leave now."

"Yes, of course," Sedela agreed.

She jumped up from the table and walked towards the door.

By the time the Marquis reached the hall she was already mounted on Flash.

They set off for Ashton House by the quickest route, which was across the fields.

It took them a little under half-an-hour to reach the Estate.

The house looked empty and somewhat sad as they rode up the drive.

"Now that Reid is dead," the Marquis said, "I hope whoever takes over here will be an asset to the neighbourhood."

"That is what I am hoping for," Sedela agreed.

"Of course, what you need is a good-looking, charming young man," the Marquis said, "who is not yet married and will undoubtedly fall in love with you!"

"That is a ridiculous idea!" she flashed back. "Since the house is large—much too large for a bachelor—the new owner will probably be middle-aged with at least half-a-dozen children."

"Then we shall have to look elsewhere for a husband for you," the Marquis remarked.

"Why are you so busy trying to marry me off?" Sedela enquired.

"Since you are more or less one of the family," the Marquis answered, "and living at my gates, I feel partly responsible for you."

"I am delighted that you should think so," Sedela said, "but I am not allowing you, or anyone else, to choose my husband for me."

"But that is what as Head of the Family I shall have to do," the Marquis argued. "In the best of families a marriage is always so that 'blood' marries 'blood,' and as you possess Windle blood, no one can deny that you qualify."

Sedela laughed.

"It all sounds very plausible," she said, "but I assure you, Ivan, I have no intention of letting you arrange my marriage any more than you would allow me to arrange yours!"

As she spoke, the Marquis could not help remembering she had in fact "dis-arranged" his.

He knew she was thinking the same thing.

They rode on in silence, the Marquis thinking:

'I will not have Esther intruding on me in everything I say and everything I think. I made a mistake, and now I have to forget it!'

At the same time, he was determined to be very, very careful whom he did marry.

It was inevitable that he should do so sooner or later, for he had to have an heir.

His father had always regretted that he had had only one son.

'I should have had three or four brothers,' the Marquis thought.

'Then there would not be the urgency for me to carry on the family name.'

But it was something he had to do.

It was unthinkable that after the Windles had succeeded from father to son for centuries the line should end with him.

It was something he should have thought about more seriously.

Instead, he had been swept off his feet by Esther's beauty and passionate appeal.

He had not considered whether she had the right type of character to be his wife.

"I was a fool, a complete fool!" the Marquis

reproached himself. "But it is something that will not happen again!"

They rode into the stable-yard of Ashton House, and a man who was obviously the Head Groom looked at them.

Then, as the Marquis dismounted, he grinned and said:

" 'Afternoon, M'Lord! Oi thinks that ye'd be a-payin' us a visit."

"You know me!" he asked. "Should I know you?"

"Oi be Wilkins, M'Lord, as started as a lad in Your Lordship's stable."

"Of course!" the Marquis exclaimed. "I thought I knew your face, but you are much older than the last time I saw you."

Wilkins laughed.

"That be true, M'Lord. Oi 'ad the opportunity of comin' 'ere when Mr. Reid first arroive, an' 'Is late Lordship give me such a good reference that 'e took me on straight away."

"I am quite sure you served him very well, Wilkins," the Marquis said, "and I would like to have a look at the horses."

"If they don' please Yer Lordship, Oi be very surprised."

He touched his forelock to Sedela, saying:

"Oi knows it were ye, Miss Sedela, as told 'Is Lordship t' come over, but Oi never 'spected 'un so soon!"

"The sooner the better!" Sedela said. "As you are aware, there is plenty of room for new horses at Windle Court."

Going to the stables, the Marquis found that

Sedela had not exaggerated when she had told him the horses were worth buying.

Reid, being a wealthy man, had bought the best.

Those he had acquired as yearlings had, over the past few years, become outstanding.

The Marquis selected six horses he wished to buy.

He agreed to the price Wilkins asked for them without any persuasion.

The man was obviously delighted at having made a sale.

The Marquis expected, however, the Executors might not be best pleased.

It was a mistake to withdraw outstanding horses before a Public Auction.

"I tell you what I will do," the Marquis said. "There are a number of horses in my stable which are now a little too old for what I require of them, but are still capable of several years of work that is not too strenuous."

"Oi knows 'xctly what ye means, M'Lord," Wilkins said, "an' it'd be a good idea t' put 'em under th' 'ammer."

"Right," the Marquis said. "I will send them over for you to-morrow."

He walked towards Flash.

Then he said:

"By the way, if you are looking for a job, Wilkins, I would be happy to have you back at the Court as long as you are prepared to work for a year or two under Barker, who will, I think, be retiring when he is sixty-five."

Wilkins gave a gasp.

"Oi'd rather come back t' Windle Court than

go anywhere else, M'Lord! Me family be in t' village and it'll be jus' loik comin' 'ome."

"Well, that is settled," the Marquis smiled.

As soon as they rode away, Sedela said:

"That was wonderful of you! I know Wilkins would rather come back to you than go to some other employer, but I did not like to suggest it, in case you thought I was intruding."

The Marquis laughed.

"I think I had better make it clear, once and for all, Sedela, that you have set yourself the task of helping me re-establish myself in the way I properly should. Therefore nothing you say or do to help me can be anything but the action of one member of the family on behalf of another."

Sedela made a murmur of delight.

"That is what I wanted you to say," she said, "but I warn you, there is a difficult task ahead of you, and you must not blame me if I ask too much."

"If you are too hard a Task-Master," the Marquis replied, "I can always leave for London and the glittering lights!"

It flashed through his mind as he did so that Esther would be waiting for him.

Then he was annoyed with himself for thinking of what he was trying to forget.

"I will keep you here," he heard Sedela say, "even if I have to chain you to the ground in order to do so!"

* * *

Lady Esther walked into her Drawing-Room with a bundle of letters in her hand.

94

She had picked them up off the hall-table when she entered the house.

She looked at them one by one.

She did not open them, but threw them down on a table with an air of disgust.

She had reached the last one when Lord Bayford came in.

"Oh, there you are, Roger!" she exclaimed. "Any news?"

"Nothing different from what you have heard before," Lord Bayford replied. "I called at Windle House and was told that His Lordship was in the country on family business and his Secretary had received no instructions as to when he would be returning."

"It is intolerable!" Lady Esther cried. "You know as well as I do that Ivan will be bored in the country, and he cannot stay there for ever just to avoid me!"

"I suppose there has been no answer to your letters?" Lord Bayford enquired.

"Not a sign of one," Lady Esther said, pointing at the pile of letters on the table.

She walked across the room and back again.

She was looking exquisitely lovely, Lord Bayford thought.

Her green gown accentuated the whiteness of her skin.

Her bonnet was trimmed with ostrich feathers and haloed her beautiful face.

He thought it was extraordinary that Windlesham, who had been obviously obsessed with Esther, could discard her so easily.

He had, of course, intruded upon them together in a very unfortunate manner.

But, after all, she was a widow, and he could hardly have expected her to remain completely celibate.

It should not be difficult for him to forgive one small indiscretion.

Lady Esther stopped moving about and sat down on the sofa.

"What are we to do, Roger?" she asked in a helpless tone.

"I have not the slightest idea," he answered. "All I know is that if I cannot get some money by some means or another, I will undoubtedly end up in the Debtors' Prison."

"You made quite a lot out of Ivan," Lady Esther said.

"Not enough for me!" Lord Bayford replied. "What I was looking forward to was your marrying him."

"I cannot believe," Lady Esther said as if she had not been listening, "that Ivan is just sitting in the country with nothing to do except admire the flowers, with no-one to talk to. You are quite sure he has not got a house-party?"

"As sure as one can be of anything," Lord Bayford replied. "All his friends are enquiring about him and the Prince Regent keeps asking when he is coming back."

"There must be something going on we do not know about," Lady Esther said. "If only we knew someone down there we could ask."

"I have not been to Windle Court since I was at Eton and stayed with Ivan in the holidays," Lord Bayford said. "I was, in fact, looking forward to going there again now that he's back from France and was ready to arrange some very amusing parties for him."

"That should be my prerogative," Lady Esther murmured.

Suddenly she gave a scream, and Lord Bayford started.

"What is it? What is the matter?" he asked.

"I have thought of something," she replied, "and I cannot imagine why I did not think of it before."

"What have you thought of? What are you talking about?" Lord Bayford asked.

"I have just recalled Ivan was telling me once how he was brought up. He said he had an old Nanny who had looked after him and of whom, like all children, he was very fond."

Lord Bayford was listening, but not with any enthusiasm.

"I remember telling Ivan that I, too, had a Nanny who died a few years ago," Lady Esther went on. "I said to him 'I suppose yours is dead too?'

" 'Not at all,' Ivan replied. 'She is very much alive, and after looking after the child of a friend of my parents she is now back at the Court, waiting for me to start a family.'

"He smiled as he spoke," Lady Esther related, "and I thought he might at that point ask me to marry him. But all he said was:

" 'I believe your Lady's-Maid is some relation of hers. A few days ago when I met her in the corridor she asked me if I had seen Nanny since I came home.' "

Lady Esther stopped speaking, and Lord Bayford exclaimed:

"Your Lady's-Maid? Well, that might be useful! Find out from her what Ivan is doing. If she does not know, persuade her to write to his old Nanny. More than likely you will hear nothing, but one never knows."

"One never knows!" Lady Esther said slowly. "And we cannot leave a stone unturned to get Ivan back!"

chapter five

WHEN she was dressing for dinner, Lady Esther said to Lucy as casually as she could make it sound:

"I understand that the Marquis of Windlesham has living at Windle Court his old Nanny, and she is some relation of yours."

There was a pause before Lucy replied:

"Yes, M'Lady."

"How interesting," Lady Esther said. "Do you often hear from her?"

"Oh, no, M'Lady," Lucy said quickly.

Lady Esther was quite certain she was lying.

She could not, however, think what she could do about it.

She therefore said no more, but thought that somehow, sooner or later, she would trap Lucy in some way.

In the meantime, she wrote several frantic letters to the Marquis, all of which remained unanswered.

She also asked a number of her friends to call at Windle House to hear if there was any news of him.

There had been none.

As the days passed, Lady Esther began to be more and more anxious.

"He will have to come back sometime," she told Lord Bayford for the hundredth time. "Only last night when I was at Carlton House His Royal Highness said:

" 'What has happened to your young man?'

" 'He is in the country, Sir,' I replied, 'and finding the cabbages so alluring that I am afraid he had forgotten me!' "

"I suppose 'Prinny' laughed at that!" Lord Bayford said.

"Oh, heartily!" Lady Esther snapped. "But I felt like screaming."

"As you say," Roger Bayford remarked, "he will have to come back sometime. I am sure the Prime Minister wants him, even if he has done all that was required from him at the War Office."

"Can we manage until he does return?" Esther asked.

"Not really," Lord Bayford answered. "I have got a commission from one of the new members of Whites, a rather stupid boy who has just come to London. It will help a bit."

"You are so clever, Roger," Lady Esther said, "that you deserve to have money—you do really!"

"That is what I think," Lord Bayford agreed, "but Fate seems to decree otherwise."

The following day Fate moved in Lady Esther's favour.

She was passing through the hall when she realised the Postman was at the door.

He was handing over a pile of letters to one of the footmen.

He took it from the man and shut the door.

Then he put the letters down on the table and started to walk towards the Pantry.

"Where are you going?" Lady Esther asked.

"Oi'm goin' t' fetch Mr. Burke, M'Lady, ter sort out th' letters."

Lady Esther did not say anything.

She knew he was unable to sort them himself because he could not read.

As he ran down the passage, she went to the table to turn over the letters.

There were several invitations as well as a number of letters from friends whose handwriting she recognised.

There was, however, nothing from the Marquis.

Then at the bottom of the pile she saw a letter addressed to Lucy.

She picked it up.

Swiftly, because she heard footsteps which were doubtless those of the Butler, she hurried up the stairs.

Her bed-room was empty and she locked the door.

Very, very carefully she opened the envelope addressed to her Lady's-Maid.

She realised as she read the address at the top of the thin paper that it was from the Marquis's Nanny.

It was what she wanted.

Nanny's father had been the village Schoolmaster.

She wrote and spelt far better than her niece.

Her hand-writing was rounded and neat.

Because she was used to reading books to the children, she had looked after she could express herself well.

Lady Esther read:

My dear Lucy,

Thank you for your long letter which I found very worrying.

However, things have altered a great deal since you wrote.

His Lordship came home and announced his intention of staying in the country, which has delighted everyone.

What is more, Miss Sedela has persuaded him to give a large party not only for the Gentry but for everyone who lives in his villages.

It takes place next Saturday and you'll hardly believe it, but there's to be a Circus, one of the big ones which has lions and tigers, snakes and monkeys. Things as we've never seen in these parts before.

On top of that there's to be Fireworks which no one except Yours Truly has ever caught a sight of before.

Anyway, you can imagine the excitement, and it's all due to Miss Sedela, who's arranging everything, with of course His Lordship's approval. We all knows how clever he is at planning a campaign, whether it be troops or just people like us.

Anyway, Dear, I think we needn't worry any more that he might marry Lady E, and we can thank God for that!

Take care of yourself and write again soon,
With love from your affectionate
Aunt Mary

Lady Esther read the letter slowly so that she would remember every word.

Then she re-sealed it.

When she went downstairs, she sent the footman on an errand.

When he was gone, she threw the letter onto the floor under the table.

It looked as if it had fallen there.

She then went into the Drawing-Room and waited for Lord Bayford.

He had promised to come to luncheon.

That was, however, in the early hours of the morning, when he was tired, and she hoped he had not forgotten, in which case she would have to send for him later.

Her fears were, however, groundless, for at a quarter-to-one he was announced.

"Good-morning, Esther," he said, coming into the room.

He was looking, considering he had had very little sleep, surprisingly fresh.

"How nice to see you, Roger," Lady Esther replied.

Then, as the Butler shut the door, she said excitedly:

"I have news to tell you and it is very important!"

Before she could say any more, the Butler returned.

He was carrying a silver tray on which was a bottle of champagne and two glasses.

While he poured out the wine, Esther and Lord Bayford talked about the weather.

They also discussed a party to which they were invited that evening.

When at last they were alone, Lady Esther said in a low voice:

"I have found out what is going on at Windle Court, and it is obvious that Ivan has got into the hands of a designing young woman!"

"I do not believe it!" Roger Bayford exclaimed.

"It is true, and he is giving a huge party for the County and for those who work on his Estate."

"That cannot do him any particular harm," Lord Bayford said, "except that it will cost money."

"You do not understand," Lady Esther said sharply. "The letter I have read was from his old Nurse to my Lady's Maid."

"You have seen one?" Lord Bayford interrupted.

Before Lady Esther could reply, luncheon was announced and it was impossible to talk freely.

It was not until coffee had been served and Lord Bayford had accepted a glass of brandy that they were alone again.

"Now go on with what you were telling me," he said.

"I found a letter from Ivan's old Nurse written to my Lady's-Maid."

"So you opened it?"

"Of course I opened it," Esther replied. "It told

me all about a girl called Sedela who is running everything!"

"I know who she is!"

"You do?"

"Yes, of course. You remember I used to stay there when I was at Eton, and I also went there for two or three days with Ivan just before he left for Portugal."

"And you met this girl?"

Lord Bayford smiled.

"She was just a child then. She was riding one of the horses from the Marquis's stables, and I have never seen anyone, before or since, ride better."

"What did she look like?" Lady Esther asked sharply.

"Lovely!" Lord Bayford replied. "Rather like a small angel—long, fair hair, big blue eyes, and she was always laughing."

He thought for a moment before he added:

"She followed Ivan everywhere, rather like a pet dog, but he did not pay very much attention to her."

"If she was a child then," Lady Esther said, "she will be grown-up by now."

"Of course," Lord Bayford agreed. "She will be, I think, a little over eighteen."

Lady Esther's lips set in a tight line.

Then she said:

"We will have to get rid of her! Now, listen, Roger, I have an idea . . ."

* * *

The excitement over the Circus infected the whole place.

It was impossible for anyone, from the children up to the oldest grandfather, to talk of anything else.

It was the same at Windle Court.

Nanny and Hanson had seen Circuses in their time.

None of the younger servants had seen one, living as they did in such a remote part of the country.

Also, during the war, most of the Travelling Circuses kept nearer to London.

It was more lucrative, and they went south, where the population was thicker.

Besides the Circus, no one had ever seen fireworks.

Sedela was determined that the party should be worthy of Ivan's bravery, something everybody present would remember for the rest of their lives.

"If I am costing you a lot of money," she said to him, "remember the years when, if you had been at home, you would have given Balls, Steeple-Chases, or Point-to-Points."

She smiled and added:

"And undoubtedly a lot of noisy house-parties where your guests would have drunk the cellars dry. All that would have cost money!"

The Marquis laughed.

"I doubt if I would have done anything of the sort! But I have given you *carte-blanche* and I am not complaining."

He was beginning to be enthusiastic himself.

It was such a pleasure to see the smiles on the faces of everyone he met.

Nanny approved of everything.

"You're doing what I told you to do, Master Ivan," she said. "You're making a lot of people happy, and no one could ask more."

"You know I always obey you, Nanny!" the Marquis teased.

"Get along with you!" Nanny replied. "You were the naughtiest child I ever had, but there was no real wickedness in you! What was more, you always said you were sorry if you'd done anything wrong."

The Marquis wondered if he should tell her he was sorry for ever having become embroiled with Lady Esther.

He had discovered, quite by chance, how Sedela had learnt about her.

He told himself he had been rather obtuse in not guessing it before.

Sedela had told him it was Nanny's birthday the following day.

"She will be sixty," she said, "and I have a special present for her."

"What you are really trying to find out," the Marquis replied, "is what I am going to give her."

"I have thought of that," Sedela said, "and I know she will be thrilled that you have remembered her."

"*You* have!" The Marquis smiled. "I am beginning to wonder how I ever ran my life without you. I am sure you would have been a great help in the Peninsula."

Sedela laughed.

"A woman on the battlefield would certainly be original. Perhaps I would go down in history as being the first since the Amazons to have ventured into the firing-line."

The Marquis did not say anything.

She had no knowledge of the "Camp Followers," who were usually just the poorest type of prostitutes.

They were a tremendous nuisance.

He had spent a great deal of time warning his men against them.

However, it was a subject he did not wish to pursue, so he simply asked:

"Now, tell me—what does Nanny want?"

"She wants a portrait of you. As you well know, you are the most important person in her life."

"A portrait?" the Marquis questioned.

"I thought," Sedela said, "although perhaps I have no right to suggest it, that the miniature in the drawer in your mother's *Secrétaire* could go up to the Nursery."

The Marquis looked at her in surprise.

"Is there a miniature there? If there is, I had no idea of it."

"Of course there is," Sedela replied. "It has been there ever since I can remember, and your mother loved it because it was painted when you were three. She said you were the most beautiful child she had ever seen."

"Show it to me," the Marquis said.

They went into the Blue Salon, and Sedela opened a drawer in the *Secrétaire*.

The Marquis remembered it as the desk at which his mother had always sat to write her letters.

It was a fine piece of French furniture that had been brought from France soon after the Revolution.

The French had sold a great many valuables confiscated from the aristocrats.

One of the Windles who was a Diplomat had brought it back to England with him.

In the drawer were a number of letters.

Some of them were tied up with blue ribbon.

Amongst them was the miniature which Sedela had been talking about.

The Marquis saw it was very well painted.

He knew there were several other portraits of him at different ages besides the one over the mantelpiece.

"Of course Nanny can have this," he said. "I will pack it up and give it to her first thing in the morning."

"I think she will have quite a lot of presents," Sedela answered, "as everybody in the house is so fond of her. But yours will be the one which will delight her more than anything else."

The Marquis found Sedela had been right.

When he went up to see Nanny, there were at least a dozen parcels on the Nursery table.

When she opened his, she gave a cry of joy, and there were tears in her eyes.

"You couldn't, Master Ivan, have given me anything I want more," she said, "and it's difficult to tell you how grateful I am."

"I know a lot of people will be thinking of you to-day, Nanny," the Marquis said, looking at the presents on the table. "I have never asked you before, but have you any relatives still alive?"

"Not many, M'Lord," Nanny answered. "I had a sister who passed away two years ago, but her daughter, Lucy, has remembered me and she's working in London."

The Marquis thought the name was familiar.

Then as Nanny went on describing two cousins whom she had not seen for years, he remembered the name of Lady Esther's Lady's-Maid.

He had thought she was rather a nice-looking woman.

He knew now how Sedela had learnt of Esther's determination to marry him.

He did not say anything because he thought it would be a mistake.

He only hoped that if Nanny wrote letters to her niece, she was discreet about what was happening here.

He had no wish for Esther to be aware of anything he was doing, for his perception told him that she would never give up her pursuit of him without a struggle.

His Secretary in London was sending him letters almost every day.

The invitations had *Refused* written on them.

Other communications and bills were marked *Answered*.

The only letters he had not opened had come from Lady Esther.

He knew her hand-writing all too well.

The Marquis was also familiar with the seductive, exotic perfume she used on herself.

It permeated the paper on which she wrote.

He did not open her letters—he merely tore them up into small pieces.

He put them in a drawer of his desk.

He did not throw them into the wastepaper basket.

He had learnt during the war to trust no one.

He felt certain that nobody in his home would betray him.

Yet he was aware that servants, like most people, were insatiably curious.

When it was cold enough to light the fires he would burn the pieces of the letters that Esther had written to him.

Until then they would remain in a locked drawer, where no one could piece them together like a jigsaw puzzle.

He left the Nursery and went downstairs to find Sedela arranging where the Circus-Tent should be set up.

It had already arrived, having come up the drive from the village.

Already the Gate-keepers were having difficulty in keeping small boys from invading the Park.

"You must explain to them," the Marquis said to one of the Gate-keepers, "that they will see everything in time, and I will not have them putting their hands through the cages of the lions and tigers, or trying to ride the elephants."

"Your Lordship's" avin' a elephant?" the Gate-keeper asked in awe.

The Marquis thought to himself that he looked like a small boy being given an unexpected treat.

When the men who had come to ask where to erect the Big Tent had left her, Sedela said:

"We are very lucky! They have just been telling me about the animals they have brought with them, and I am finding it difficult not to rush out and see them at once!"

"I feel rather the same," the Marquis said, smiling. "It is a long time since I saw a Circus."

He thought back into the past before he went on:

"My father took me once to Astley's Circus in London. I remember being thrilled by the horses and, of course, the lions and tigers."

"I saw one in St. Albans," Sedela said. "It was not a very good one, but Papa and Mama took me as a Christmas treat. I think I was more thrilled by the monkeys than anything else."

"Then we will make certain," the Marquis said, "that whoever else has a good seat in the Big Top, you and I will have the best. Anyway, it is what we deserve after all the trouble we have taken!"

"Just in case it rains," Sedela said, "I am arranging tea in the Ball-Room for your guests from the County who disdain going to anything as vulgar as a Circus, and prefer to stay on the green lawns."

"I will definitely be with the *hoi polloi* in the Big Top!" the Marquis said firmly.

Sedela laughed.

"I would not be surprised to find you riding round the ring performing on one of the horses, or joining in with the Clowns!"

"Perhaps that is what I am best suited for!" the Marquis said.

He waited for Sedela to contradict him.

Any other woman would have protested that he was far too clever for that.

Instead, Sedela laughed.

"If you think yourself a Clown, that is exactly what you will be."

"If you talk like that," the Marquis said, "I will forget how old you are and give you a good spanking!"

"I think that is unlikely," Sedela answered. "Now that you are so important, you have to behave like a Gentleman, whether you like it or not!"

She looked at him as she spoke in a provocative way from under her eye-lashes.

It was an entirely artless gesture which he remembered she used to make as a child.

It struck him it was a pity she had grown up.

He knew he had never met in London, in France, or anywhere else, any woman so unself-conscious or so completely ignorant of her own charms.

He found himself thinking that if she went to London, she would be a sensation.

Properly dressed, chaperoned by somebody of importance, she would take the *Beau Monde* by storm.

Then, he thought, it would spoil her.

He could not bear to think of her flirting as Esther did with every man she met.

He did not want Sedela's artless way of talking to be changed into the affected language of the *Beau Monde*, where every other sentence contained a *double entendre*.

'She must stay as she is!' he thought determinedly.

Then he wondered if, after to-morrow, that would be possible.

Amongst the multitude of people who had been asked to his party, there would be a number of men of about the same age as himself.

Their names, which he had forgotten until he read them, were on the list Sedela had given him.

Their parents lived in the country, but they had been in London enjoying the "Social Round."

At least half-a-dozen of them were members of Whites Club.

Abruptly he asked:

"What are you going to wear to-morrow?"

He saw that Sedela looked surprised at his question.

"A new gown," she replied, "which Nanny has made for me from some material of my mother's, and it is very, very pretty!"

She paused before she asked:

"Are you afraid of being ashamed of me?"

"No, of course not," the Marquis answered. "I had just thought it was something I should have asked before, and perhaps given you one as a present."

"It is very kind of you to think of it," Sedela said, "but Nanny was insistent that I look smart, and she has been working until midnight every night. So mind you tell her, no matter what you really think, that I looked nice."

The Marquis thought that would certainly be an understatement.

Smiling, he said:

"Let us get luncheon over as soon as possible so that we can go and see how the Circus is getting on."

"I expect we shall find that a crowd of small boys have managed to clamber over the walls and they will behave only if you take command," Sedela said.

"I thought I would not be allowed to have a moment to myself!" the Marquis complained.

"I have never known you with nothing to do," Sedela said, "and the day that does happen, I think you will find you have become a very old man walking with a stick!"

The Marquis was laughing as they went into the Dining-Room.

It suddenly occurred to him that every meal they had together was always very amusing.

He had come down to the country bitter, angry, and furious with himself.

He had found his first meals which he had taken alone were, to put it mildly, gloomy.

Then, because he had so many things to discuss with her, he had invited Sedela to join him.

Time seemed to fly by.

There were not enough hours in the day to get through everything that had to be done.

There were so many questions to be asked, so many decisions to be made.

It was only after tea and before she went home to dinner that they had a chance of talking of other things that interested them.

The Marquis was not surprised to find how well-read Sedela was.

He had always known that the General was an extremely clever and cultured man.

He soon found that Sedela had been far better educated than most young women of her age.

Sedela had an informed opinion on every subject, besides usually a number of intelligent and interesting suggestions to make, especially where it concerned him.

"You must make a speech about this," she would say. "They would listen to you in the House of Lords if you told them how badly that particular Law works out in the country, however it may in the City."

He knew he had never had such conversations with Esther or with any of the other women with whom he had ever been involved.

When he had not been making love to them, there had been intervals of boredom.

Sedela had been quite right in thinking the boys of the village would have discovered the Circus before they reached it.

There was a crowd of them looking at the caged animals and watching the Big Top being erected by the Circus hands.

When they saw the Marquis coming, they hurriedly slipped away behind the bushes.

"Shall I drive them off?" he asked Sedela.

"You could not be so cruel," she answered. "They are so thrilled by what they are seeing, and so am I! We cannot be selfish and keep it all to ourselves."

They walked towards the men who were coping with the tent.

The Proprietor came out to greet the Marquis.

He was a handsome man.

Sedela knew he would look very much the part when he appeared in his top hat and red coat to introduce the various acts.

"I've got some very original items t' show Your Lordship," he was saying to the Marquis, "including a Snake-Charmer, which I've added to th' 'Turns,' and I likes to think it's what no other Circus 'as at th' moment."

"Why is that?" asked the Marquis.

"Your Lordship knows better than anyone else there's been no chance of 'aving any ships in from th' East while them 'Frenchies' were ready t' sink anythin' that carried th' British flag."

"Thanks to Lord Nelson, they did not succeed." The Marquis smiled.

"That be true enough," the Circus-owner replied, "and now we've got some new animals. M' tiger's a real fine one, as Your Lordship 'll see, an' a young elephant's replaced th' old 'un that died three years ago."

He took them proudly to see his animals.

Sedela loved the tiger and the lions which were also new.

There were monkeys which had arrived on a ship from South Africa only two months ago.

Also a black panther from India which, the Proprietor told them, was very dangerous.

The Marquis was interested to see the horses, which he acknowledged were outstanding.

"I am certainly very grateful to you," he said to the Proprietor when they had inspected everything, "for coming so far off your usual track."

"It's a pleasure, Your Lordship," he replied.

They walked back towards the House.

Sedela was aware that as they left, the small boys came creeping out from behind the bushes.

She was not surprised that they were thrilled.

She knew that the Circus was a far better one than she had dared to anticipate.

"We are lucky to have got it," she said to the Marquis.

"I agree," he replied, "but I am not going to ask you what it is costing."

"A lot of money, but you cannot count in hard cash the pleasure it will give to the children, if no one else."

"And, of course, to you!" the Marquis said.

"I am thrilled, delighted, entranced!" Sedela flashed.

"One day you will have to grow up."

"Not until I have seen the Circus!" she answered quickly.

The Marquis laughed again.

When they reached the House, they found the guests who were staying with the Marquis had begun to arrive.

Here again Sedela had remembered which of his relations were the most important and who would be extremely indignant and upset if they were forgotten.

Because his house-party consisted entirely of his relatives, they accepted Sedela as one of themselves.

"I am so sorry to hear," one of the Marquis's elderly aunts said to her, "that your dear mother and father cannot be here. I do hope that your aunt recovers soon."

She bent forward to kiss her.

"I am so glad to see you again, my dear," she went on. "You were always such a pretty and delightful child."

Because the Marquis had insisted on it, Sedela had moved into Windle Court for the party.

"There are a thousand things to see to with so many staying with me," he said, "and you know I have no hostess. You can look after their comforts far better than anybody else can."

"Of course I will, if you want me to," Sedela said.

"Then let me make it quite clear that I do want you!" the Marquis answered.

She was delighted at being needed by him.

She ran upstairs to tell Nanny the good news.

"What do you think, Nanny?" she asked. "Ivan has asked me to stay here when his relations arrive to-morrow. I have already told the housemaids to make me up a bed here next to you."

"That's a good idea, Miss Sedela," Nanny said, "and you know I would like to have you."

"I want to make certain of that, Nanny," said Sedela, "since it is Ivan who is getting all your attention, and I am jealous!"

"There's no need for you to be," Nanny said sharply. "Love's not a cake which you can cut into pieces so that if someone has too big a slice, the others starve."

Sedela had heard Nanny say this before.

She smiled as Nanny went on:

"There's enough love in me for you, for Master Ivan, and a dozen others, and the sooner they arrive, the better!"

Sedela laughed.

She knew that Nanny was once again referring to Ivan getting married and having babies.

She looked over her shoulder before she said in a low voice:

"I think he is happy again, Nanny, and has forgotten that woman who upset him."

"And so I should hope!" Nanny said. "But I don't trust her, and that's a fact!"

Sedela looked anxious.

"What do you mean?"

"I had a letter from Lucy this morning and she told me she's planning something—Lucy doesn't know what—but she knows it's something to do with Master Ivan."

"Oh, Nanny, I hope not!" Sedela cried. "He is just like his old self again now."

She sighed before she went on:

"When he first came home he kept thinking about her. I could see it in his eyes and sense the anger and bitterness coming from him."

"That's what I feared," Nanny murmured.

"Now he is quite different," Sedela went on, "and I am sure he is not thinking of her, even at night. Although he pretends not to, he is enjoying every minute of the excitement over the Circus and the party."

Nanny put her hand on Sedela's shoulder.

"You've done your best, dearie," Nanny said, "an' no one could do more."

"I want him to be happy," Sedela said, "and I'm sure he is no longer in danger, or he would have seen Lady Constance."

"Now, don't go talking like that!" Nanny said. "It gives me the creeps, as I've told you before."

Sedela remembered how upset Nanny had been when she had last seen Lady Constance.

That was just before the old Marquis had died.

"Ivan is happy," she said quickly, "and all we have to do is to enjoy ourselves at the Circus. I know that you, Nanny, will be thrilled with it. I will go down first thing to-morrow and put *Reserved* on a special seat for you."

"That's very thoughtful of you," Nanny said. "I wouldn't want to miss seeing that Snake-Charmer! I've heard about those men in India, but I've never seen one."

"I am more interested in the black panther," Sedela said. "It is the most beautiful animal I have ever seen!"

"Now all you've got to do is to look beautiful yourself." Nanny smiled. "Your gown is finished and I was going to send one of the maids over with it."

"She will not have far to go, Nanny, now that I will be next door to you, and you can button it up and make sure it fits me!"

"I'd defy anyone to find anything wrong with it!" Nanny said sharply.

Then she realised that Sedela was teasing her.

"You'll be the *Belle* of the Party, Miss Sedela!" she said. "I've also changed the flowers on your bonnet and added a few that I had by me."

"Oh, thank you, Nanny, thank you!"

Sedela kissed Nanny, then ran hastily downstairs to see if Ivan wanted her for anything.

'I am happy . . . I have never been so happy,' she thought. 'Oh, please, God, do not let that wicked woman in London upset it all . . . or hurt him!'

It was a fervent prayer that came from the depths of her heart.

chapter six

THE applause in the Big Top was deafening.

Sedela, looking at the happy faces of the children, knew it was a huge success.

The monkeys climbed up and down the poles, and their antics caused shrieks of laughter.

The lions, while in fact quite quiet, seemed, like the tigers, terrifying enough as they padded round the ring.

The snakes moved obediently in response to the Indian's pipe.

They were watched with an awe which kept everybody silent.

The greatest success was the elephant.

It was not a very large one, but the children found him fascinating, especially when the Clowns came in riding or falling off his back.

The Marquis and Sedela had organised everything down to the last detail.

The Circus performance started at five o'clock and ended at half-past six.

Those elderly people, and there were only a few of them, who did not want to attend, sat in the garden or else moved into the house.

It was a lovely day with brilliant sunshine, yet not so hot that anyone was uncomfortable.

When the Circus performance was over, the villagers and those who lived on the Estate moved into two huge tents.

They had been erected in the field next to the garden.

There was a great deal for them to eat.

The Marquis had provided huge barrels of ale and cider to quench their thirst.

The rest of the party, and the Marquis's relatives and friends, moved up to the house.

They rested in the Drawing-Room, where they were served champagne.

Dinner, they were told, would be at quarter-past-eight in the large Dinning-Room.

The members of the house-party went upstairs to change.

The younger people were not to eat in the Dining-Room but in the Ball-Room.

There was a Buffet there and a small Orchestra to which they could dance if they wished.

Sedela came downstairs wearing the pretty evening gown which Nanny had made for her.

She could hear the music and half-wished she could dance to it in the Ball-Room.

But the Marquis had been insistent that she should be in the Dining-Room.

She thought it would be greedy of her to want anything more.

Everybody was in a good humour.

The Marquis's relations were all thrilled to have him home.

His oldest aunt, who was in her sixties, acted as hostess at Dinner.

The party filled not only the large table in the centre of the room.

A number of smaller tables had had to be erected in order to accommodate them all.

They ate a delicious meal which Mrs. Benson and a whole posse of assistant cooks had provided.

Looking round as they did so, Sedela thought nothing could have gone off better.

As the meal finished, she thought that the most exciting moment of the whole day would begin when it was dusk.

The Marquis's aunt gave the signal for the ladies to leave the gentlemen.

But as they rose the Marquis said:

"I think it would be best if we all took our places, which have been arranged, for the Fireworks. As I am supervising their being let off, I must ask you gentlemen to forgive me if we do not pass round the port to-night."

As they had already had a generous number of wines to drink, there was no protect at this.

The Marquis and the other gentlemen left the Dining-Room with the ladies.

They reached the hall.

As they did so, the Marquis saw that somebody had just driven up outside and was coming in through the front-door.

As Sedela looked at the newcomer, she realised she was the most beautiful woman she had ever seen.

She was dazzling in the amount of jewellery she wore.

There was a bandeau of diamonds round her hair, which had touches of red in it.

She wore a necklace of the same stones and bracelets which shimmered with every movement she made.

Sedela wondered who the newcomer was.

Then she was aware that the Marquis, who was only a few steps ahead of her, had stiffened and was standing still.

The uninvited guest ran towards him.

"Ivan!" she exclaimed. "How could you give a party without me? I would have been here earlier, but it took longer from London than I anticipated. Say you are pleased to see me!"

It was then Sedela realised this was undoubtedly Lady Esther Hasting.

She looked at the Marqius apprehensively.

It hurt her to see there was anger in his eyes.

The bitterness was back in the tightness of his lips and the expression on his face.

Even as he felt the fury rising within him, the Marquis knew it would be a mistake to have a scene in front of his relatives.

He had earlier become aware that a number of them were surprised when they arrived to find she was not included in the party.

They had, however, been too tactful to ask why she was not there.

Esther, having greeted him, was looking up at him.

She was well aware she glittered like a peacock amongst a number of ordinary birds.

In a firm, controlled voice that Sedela admired, the Marquis said slowly:

126

"I am afraid, Esther, you are too late for dinner. We have just finished."

"I am not hungry," Esther replied, "just thrilled to see you again, and to be here among so many old friends."

She moved as she spoke towards several of the Marquis's relatives, kissing them affectionately.

She was saying flattering if gushing things to them.

She made it impossible for them to accept her graciously.

"I hear to-night you have Fireworks!" she said in a lilting voice. "How delightful! And what could be a more perfect setting for them?"

There was no answer to this, and the Marquis walked swiftly through the front-door.

Sedela knew he was making straight for the other side of the lake.

The Fireworks were ready, the men only waiting for the order to begin.

It was not yet quite dark enough.

The sun had only just set, and the first evening stars were coming out in the sky.

It had been the Marquis's idea to set them up on the other side of the lake against the background of the great oak trees in the Park.

He had pointed out to Sedela that as they burnt themselves out, they would fall into the lake and harm no one.

"I am always afraid when there are Fireworks that the children who are staring up at them might receive an eye injury."

"It is clever of you to think of that," Sedela agreed, "and of course you are right."

The Fireworks, and there were a great number of them, were therefore arranged on the farther bank of the lake.

Those who had been eating and drinking in the tents were to sit on the grass on the near side.

From there the ground sloped up to the level of the court-yard in front of the house.

Here a large number of chairs had been placed for the guests the Marquis had entertained for dinner.

As they moved towards the chairs, Lady Esther went with them.

Watching her, Sedela had to admit to herself that she was indeed exceptionally beautiful.

She wondered if seeing her again would make the Marquis forgive her.

She knew, however, that if he did so, he would once more be in danger.

Whatever else Lady Esther might be, Sedela was convinced that she was evil.

She could not explain how she knew this.

But it vibrated out from her, even though every word she spoke was honeyed and charming.

If he did go back to her, Sedela thought, he would be hurt.

Although he might not think so at the time, it would inevitably ruin his life.

She sent up a frantic prayer that the Marquis would be saved.

She was only thankful that at this moment he was on the other side of the lake.

It was therefore impossible for Lady Esther to get near him.

It took some time to get everybody seated.

Sedela made certain that the most elderly of the Marquis's relatives were comfortable.

At the same time, she was acutely aware of Lady Esther.

It grew darker, but her diamonds still seemed to be twinkling like the stars which were now filling the sky.

Then at last the first Firework shot up from the ground, and as it burst, its light was reflected in the lake.

There was a wild cry of delight from the children.

The Marquis let the Fireworks off one after another.

They were certainly very beautiful.

Of every possible colour, they poured down like falling stars.

Finally they sizzled out harmlessly in the water.

There were also Fireworks which, set up on the bank, looked when they were ignited like a golden or silver fountain.

There were others which zoomed up into the sky making a screeching noise.

They vanished in a stream of colour.

It was very exciting and everybody watching the performance was enthralled.

The display had lasted for about twenty minutes, when a footman came to Sedela's side.

"There's bin an accident, Miss Sedela!" he said in a low voice.

"An accident?" she exclaimed.

"I thinks as 'ow you'd better come at once, Miss!"

"Yes . . . of course."

She rose from the chair in which she had been sitting.

Without saying anything to the two elderly ladies sitting on each side of her, she followed the footman.

He had already moved away from her.

As she hurried, running behind him, she noticed he was not wearing livery of any sort.

She thought he must be one of the temporary servants whom Hanson had hired for the evening.

There was, as she knew, a large number of extra staff, especially in the Dining-Room and kitchen.

The man continued to walk quickly ahead of her.

He hurried round the side of the house and onto the lawn.

Sedela supposed the accident must have occurred outside.

She wanted to ask him who had been injured and how.

But he was moving so quickly that she could not catch up with him.

They passed the herbaceous borders and crossed the Bowling Green.

Sedela wondered how an accident could have happened at this part of the grounds.

She suspected it must be one of the young people.

She had seen them larking about after leaving the Big Top.

That was before they went into the Ball-Room for supper.

By now the man in front of her had reached the rhododendron bushes.

They formed the first part of the shrubbery.

Sedela was now able to see him clearly because the moon had come out.

Its rays were spreading a silver light over the garden.

Sedela thought if he disappeared through the trees, she would have difficulty in following him.

She therefore quickened her pace.

As he passed through bushes she parted her lips to ask him to go a little slower.

It was then suddenly, as the leaves began to brush her bare arms, a heavy cloth was thrown over her head.

She felt herself being picked up in a man's arms.

She was so taken by surprise that for a moment she could not even cry out.

When she tried to do so, she found the cloth which covered her head was so thick that her voice was lost in it.

The man carrying her was holding her very firmly.

This combined with the shock of what had happened made it difficult for her to breathe.

Her arms were held close to her sides.

She tried to kick with her feet, but found it was impossible.

She could feel she was being carried uphill.

She thought the man was walking on a path.

There were several paths, she knew, which led through the shrubbery up into the woodland.

She could not think why this was happening to her.

But it was terrifying to realise that the man carrying her was so large and strong.

She knew it would be impossible for her to escape from him.

Suddenly he came to a standstill, and for the first time she heard her captor speak.

"Open the door!"

It was an order given in a low voice.

Then, so suddenly that she screamed, she was flung onto a floor.

The cloth that had covered her was jerked away from her body.

"Keep quiet!" a voice said harshly. "If you make a sound, you will be silenced in a manner you will find most painful!"

As the man finished speaking, he shut the door.

Sedela found herself in complete darkness.

For a moment she was too frightened to move.

Then she heard the man speaking.

She knew he was just outside the door he had slammed shut.

She could not hear what he was saying, and with an effort she rose to her feet.

Putting out her hands in front of her, she moved a few steps through the darkness.

Her fingers touched the door she had heard shut.

Now she knew where she was.

But she did not want to think about anything except to hear what the man was saying.

He was speaking in a very low voice.

She put her ear against the wood of the door and could just hear him.

"What do you mean," he was asking, "he will not let me have it?"

" 'E said, M'Lord, 'e wanted anuvver twenty pounds as them snakes be difficult to get 'old of."

As the other man spoke, Sedela knew that it was Lord Bayford who had carried her here.

She held her breath, trying to hear everything that was said.

"I have given him the money already," Lord Bayford protested angrily. "Where is he now?"

" 'E'll be at t' bottom at th' gate into th' garden."

"And he has the snake with him?"

"Aye, M'Lord."

"Damn him for his impertinent greed!" Lord Bayford swore. "I will go and get it!"

He paused, and then said:

"Now you stay here! Do not let anyone see you! If the girl tries to escape, which is unlikely, hit her on the head with this bludgeon."

"Very good, M'Lord."

"I will be as quick as I can."

Sedela heard Lord Bayford walk away, and there was silence.

Then with a feeling of indescribable horror she guessed what he intended to do.

She knew exactly where she was.

She was in a small wooden house among the trees.

It had been built for Ivan by the wood-cutters when he was a little boy.

Made from trunks of trees split in half, it had two windows, one on either side of the door.

These had strong wooden shutters over them which were closed from the outside.

The door itself had a strong lock of which Ivan had proudly kept the key.

It had been his fortress, a place that was all his own.

It was where he took his friends when he was home for the School holidays.

There they could plot anything they wanted without being disturbed.

She supposed Lord Bayford, being Ivan's friend, must have been shown the wooden house when he stayed at Windle Court as a boy.

Her intelligence told her exactly what Lady Esther and Lord Bayford were planning.

For some reason, they must have thought it was she who was preventing the Marquis from returning to London.

She must therefore be disposed of.

It was, she knew if she was honest, quite a clever plot.

Somehow Lord Bayford had found out there would be a Circus with performing snakes.

He had purchased one of the snakes.

Later it would be difficult to hold the Circus-man guilty of anything more than carelessness in letting it escape.

She would be found sometime in the wooden house dead from a snake-bite.

There would be no one to tell the Marquis how it had come about that she had been bitten by the snake.

Lord Bayford and his accomplice would have unlocked the door after her death and disappeared.

Later it would be accepted that she had gone there for some reason no one could explain.

And that the snake, which had escaped from the Circus, had been hiding there.

This all flashed through her mind.

She knew it was no use screaming or calling for help.

If she did, the accomplice on Lord Bayford's orders would strike her until she was unconscious.

'I want . . . to live . . . I must . . . live!' she thought. 'If I do not do so, once I have . . . gone they will . . . hurt Ivan.'

It was the thought of him that spurred her to try to think of some way by which she could escape.

She knew the wooden house well.

She was aware that it was impossible for the shutters to be opened from the inside.

She could not open the door either.

Now that her eyes had grown used to the gloom, she looked up.

There were small gaps in the roof through which glimmers of moonlight were showing.

She guessed that the tree-trunks had warped and shrunk over the years.

Perhaps the winds and storms of Winter had moved them a little.

She stared at the roof, wondering if she was strong enough to swing herself on to one of the cross-beams.

Then she realised that the centre of the roof was in complete darkness.

She knew why that was.

The Crest of the Windles was an arrow.

They had used it since the first Windle had been created an Earl at the Battle of Agincourt.

Thanks to being an outstanding marksman with a bow and arrow, he had saved the life of the young King Henry V.

He had swiftly shot a French archer, who had drawn a bow on the King at short range, and killed him before he could release his arrow.

It was for this he received his Earldom and took as his Crest an Arrow together with the motto: *I shoot straight*.

It had amused Ivan's father, the old Marquis, to have an arrow erected on quite a number of his buildings, even on the stables.

Ivan had demanded that he, too, should have one on his wooden house.

It was the Estate Carpenter who had put one there for him.

Unfortunately, Sedela remembered, because it involved making a small hole in the roof, the rain had seeped through.

It had soaked various books and other treasures which he kept in his wooden house.

To protect them subsequently, two flat boards had been placed under the arrow.

They rested on the two beams which were the main support of the roof itself.

It was almost as if her Guardian Angel were telling her what to do.

Sedela knew that if she could climb up onto

those flat boards, she would be safe from the snake.

The difficulty, as she knew of old, was the smooth, bare trunks of which the house was built.

Quickly, because she was frightened and knew she had but a very short time in which to save herself, she put out her hands to feel her way.

She found a chair and pushed it close against the wall.

It was an ordinary upright chair but stoutly made.

As she stood on it, she knew it would support her.

She stretched up her arms.

She still had a long way to climb to reach the roof.

She kicked off her slippers. Gripping with her hands and her stocking feet, she tried to lift herself up.

Fortunately she was very light.

She also was used to climbing up onto the back of a horse without assistance.

Moreover, the long rides she had often taken alone had kept her fit and supple.

Three times she fell back attempting to climb the wall.

She had learnt as a small child to fall from a horse without hurting herself.

So she managed to get up quickly and try again.

At last she caught hold of one of the crossbeams.

For a moment she just swung in the air.

Painstakingly, by sheer determination, she managed at last to hook one leg over it.

After that it was easy to edge her way slowly to where the wooden boards lay beneath the arrow on the roof.

The space in which she could hide was less than a foot in height.

It would have been impossible for anyone larger than she was to insert herself between the boards and the roof.

It was a very tight squeeze, but somehow she managed it.

Only when she was actually lying on the wooden boards did she feel she could breathe again.

Her heart no longer felt as if it would burst.

She was only just in position when she heard a voice outside the door.

Lord Bayford had returned.

She heard the other man give an exclamation, and Lord Bayford hushed him into silence.

Then, as she lay squeezed in her place of safety, she knew what they were about to do.

Lord Bayford was carefully untying the lid of the basket in which was the cobra he had bought from the Circus.

She heard him whisper something to his accomplice.

Then there was the sound of the key turning in the lock.

She held her breath in case he had a light with him.

If he had, he would realise she was no longer lying on the floor.

Then the door opened, but there was only a

glint of light from the moon outside.

Against it she saw the shadow of a man's arm and a basket.

She remembered one like it containing the performing snakes in the Circus.

She had watched fascinated as the cobras uncoiled themselves and rose up from the basket.

They had swayed to the sound the Indian Charmer made on his pipe.

The basket jerked and Sedela thought Lord Bayford had punched it with his fist.

Then she was aware that something had been shaken from it and was hissing in anger.

The arm and the basket disappeared and the door was slammed shut.

Lord Bayford and his accomplice did not speak.

She heard their footsteps as they hurried away.

Sedela drew in her breath.

The cobra was still hissing angrily below her, and there was the rustle of dried leaves as it slithered over them.

She tried to remember if snakes could climb, and had the idea that they could.

She shut her eyes and began to pray.

There was nothing else she could do, and she believed that God could hear her.

*   *   *

The Fireworks came to an end, and all the spectators clapped and cheered.

On the other side of the lake the Marquis thought it was a very happy sound.

He knew his party had been a great success and that it would give everybody a great deal to talk about for a long time to come.

When he came back to where his guests were sitting, they all congratulated him.

At the same time, their carriages were being brought round from the stables.

Most people were eager to get home.

It had been a satisfactory but very long day, and the elderly were tired.

The Marquis was aware that Esther was determined to talk to him alone.

He was equally determined she should not do so.

At last the guests who had arrived in carriages had almost all departed.

There was just one carriage left.

He knew it belonged to Esther.

A few minutes earlier she had been hovering behind him while he said good-bye to the Lord Lieutenant and his wife.

Now he was aware that she had gone into the Drawing-Room.

She was chatting to those of his relations who had not yet gone to bed.

"A lovely evening, Ivan!" one of his aunts said as he entered the room. "I have never known people to enjoy a party more, and it is certainly something you must do again."

"Not for several years!" the Marquis demurred.

His aunt laughed.

"I am sure we will all be begging you this time next year to have a Circus again and a Fireworks Display at the same time."

She gave a little laugh before she added:

"Although I have enjoyed it, I must admit I am now very tired."

"Go to bed, Aunt," the Marquis said. "It is what I now intend to do myself."

He was about to cross the room to say good-night to another relative when Lady Esther stopped him

"I want to talk to you, Ivan," she said softly.

"We have nothing to say to each other, Esther!" he replied firmly.

"I have a lot to say," she said in the seductive voice he knew so well.

As she spoke, she put out her hand and laid it on his arm, raising her face to his in a gesture he had once found irresistible.

The Marquis looked at her.

Quite suddenly he knew that any feelings of affection he had ever had for her had completely evaporated.

She might be beautiful, but he was no longer moved by her beauty.

He did not even admire her.

It seemed a strange and somewhat banal thing to say, but she "left him cold."

It was the falling of the curtain, the shutting-down of everything that had once been between them, and for the moment he could hardly believe it himself.

He knew, if he was honest, that he had been afraid of meeting her, afraid that the allure which he had found so fascinating would tempt him into forgiving her.

Now he knew there was no question of that,

no question of her ever again troubling him in any way, whether by arousing his anger or any other feeling.

Whatever there had been between them was dead.

He was free.

He looked down at her, and there was no expression on his face except one of complete unconcern.

"Good-night, Esther," he said, "and good-bye!"

He turned away from her as he spoke, not angrily or impatiently, but merely indifferently.

It was as if he could no longer be bothered to think about her.

As he walked across the room, she knew without his having to say so that she was defeated.

He was no longer thinking of her.

There was still, however, a flicker of hope in her mind when she remembered that Roger Bayford would be waiting for her at the end of the drive.

She would pick him up.

On their way back to London he would be able to tell her that at least his part in their cleverly constructed plan had been successful.

*   *   *

The Marquis said good-night to the rest of his relatives who were staying in the house.

Only as the last one went upstairs did he wonder what had happened to Sedela.

He had a feeling she might be outside with the villagers and the tenants.

Of course it would be very like her to be with the children.

He walked to the front-door and found that two footmen were closing it.

"Everyone's gone 'ome m'Lord," one of them said.

He looked out of a window and saw there was no light to be seen except that of the moon.

He walked towards the stairs.

Then, as he went up to the First Floor, he saw somebody waiting there.

It was Nanny.

"You are not waiting up for me, Nanny?" he asked. "I am sure it is time you had your 'Beauty sleep'!"

Nanny came nearer to him.

"Where's Miss Sedela?" she asked.

The Marquis stared at her.

"I thought she would be with you or had gone to bed a long time ago."

"She's not upstairs," Nanny said, "and one of the footmen was telling me something strange that he saw."

"What was that?" the Marquis asked.

"He was saying downstairs and laughing about it that as he was looking for a cup or something that was missing on the lawn, he sees a man carrying a woman in his arms just beyond the rhododendron bushes."

"Did he see who it was?" the Marquis asked.

Nanny shook her head.

"No, but he said the woman had on a white gown."

Nanny paused before she added:

"Miss Sedela was wearing a white gown—and there's no sign of her—and I feel worried about her, I really do!"

"By the rhododendron bushes," the Marquis said as if to himself.

He supposed two of his guests might have gone there if they wanted to kiss and cuddle each other.

But he could not imagine that Sedela would want to do anything like that.

Now he came to think about it, he had not seen her since just after dinner.

She had been helping his guests into their seats as he went across the lake to set off the Fireworks.

All he could remember was that Esther had been there.

He had thought it shocking of her to intrude on his party in the way she had.

It now suddenly struck him as unlikely that Esther would have travelled down from London alone.

She would have wanted somebody to talk to.

That meant a man.

He suspected that man would be Roger Bayford, but if he, or some other man, had come with her, no one had been aware of it.

And if it had been he whom the footman had seen, why should he be carrying Sedela?

"I'm frightened, Master Ivan," Nanny was saying, "I'm frightened for Miss Sedela! There's something wrong, I feels it in me bones!"

She hesitated for a moment, then added:

"Besides, and I know you'll laugh at me, but I swear before God that while I was waiting for her I saw Lady Constance!"

"You are frightening yourself, Nanny, and imagining things," the Marquis said quickly.

"Have you ever known me to tell a lie?" Nanny asked. "I tell you, Master Ivan, Miss Sedela's in danger and you've got to save her!"

The Marquis drew in his breath.

Then he turned and ran down the stairs and ordered the footmen to open the front-door.

As he hurried away, he looked at the rows of empty chairs on the lawn, but there was no sign of her.

He looked beyond the sloping lawn and the lake to where the Circus tents had been pitched.

There was no light from that direction.

He had noticed that the Big Top had been dismantled immediately after the performance.

He thought, although he could not be sure, that all the people from the Circus had gone.

They had, in fact, told him that they intended to move as quickly as possible.

He was, however, not interested in them, but in finding Sedela.

He walked across the lawn and past the long herbaceous borders.

He reached the rhododendrons which formed the beginning of the shrubbery.

The bushes were thick and the path between them narrow and winding.

He wondered if the man who carried off the girl had found somewhere where they could sit and cuddle unnoticed.

It was then he remembered his wooden house.

It was years since he had last been in it, but he supposed it was still standing.

It would certainly be a convenient place for lovers.

But in that case he knew the girl would not have been Sedela.

He was just about to go back again towards the house when he felt as if Sedela were calling him.

Thinking it strange, he stood still.

He thought he could hear her voice, or perhaps it was something he heard with his heart rather than with his ears.

"It is foolish," he chided himself, "but as I am here, I might as well have a look at the wooden house."

He climbed up the path towards it.

It was well hidden until he was suddenly aware of it just ahead of him.

It seemed to him to blend in with the trees.

There were a great number of saplings and small bushes which had grown up round it.

As he reached it, he could see that the shutters were closed.

He put his hand towards the door, and as he did so he heard Sedela cry out:

"Ivan . . . is that . . . you?"

"Sedela!" he exclaimed. "Where are you? What is happening?"

He grasped the handle of the door as he spoke, then as he would have turned it she screamed:

"No, Ivan! Do not . . . open the . . . door! Do not . . . touch . . . it!"

"What are you talking about?" the Marquis asked.

He, however, obeyed her because she sounded so agitated.

"There is . . . a cobra . . . a cobra inside here . . . with me . . . it has been put here to . . . k-kill me!"

chapter seven

FOR a moment the Marquis was unable to answer.

He thought what he was hearing could not be true.

Then the unmistakable terror in Sedela's voice made him say quickly:

"Where is the snake and where are you?"

"I am up on the . . . boards under the . . . roof," Sedela replied, "but I am . . . afraid he may . . . climb up the wall."

The Marquis's brain began to work as swiftly as when he was on a battlefield.

"Stay where you are and keep very quiet," he ordered.

As he spoke he turned and ran back to the house.

He ran faster than he had ever done since leaving Eton, where he had won a number of races for his House.

He tore in through the garden-door, knowing it was quicker that way to reach the Gun-Room.

He remembered that not only were guns kept there, but there were also a number of candle-lanterns.

He reached up to a lighted sconce and took the candle from it to light his way in the Gun-Room.

It gave enough light for him to be able to see what he was doing.

He opened the glass-fronted cupboard where the pistols were kept.

There were quite a number of them which had been collected over the ages: duelling-pistols that had been used by at least three or four members of the Windle family, and pistols that had been carried by Coachmen on carriages for fear of Highwaymen.

There were also pistols similar to those which the Marquis had used himself in the war.

He picked up one of these, found the bullets, and loaded it.

He was working at a speed which made him feel breathless.

He saw the candle-lanterns on top of a chest.

There were three of them.

He picked up one of them and lit it from his candle.

Then, with his pistol in his other hand, he started back the way he had come.

He dared not run quite as fast as he had on the way to the Gun-Room for fear of extinguishing the candle.

It was, however, still burning brightly when he reached the wooden house.

"Are you there, Sedela?"

As he spoke, he was desperately afraid there would be no answer.

He knew in that moment that he could not lose her.

He felt as if a cold hand clutched at his heart until he heard her say:

"Oh, Ivan . . . help me . . . I am so . . . frightened."

The Marquis held his pistol to the key-hole of the door and one shot was enough to smash the lock.

He opened the door with one hand, holding his smoking pistol with the other.

He then bent and picked up the candle-lantern to hold it high above his head.

A quick glance showed him the cobra was on the chair.

It was reaching up above the back of the chair as if it were trying to climb up to where Sedela was hiding.

With a steady movement the Marquis brought his pistol down in aim on the snake.

He pulled the trigger.

The explosion echoed round the small house, and it seemed almost to rock the walls.

There was no question of the cobra being alive.

With the true aim of a first-class shot, the Marquis had shattered its head.

The snake's body fell to the ground, the tail twitching until at last it was still.

The Marquis put down his pistol and held up the lantern.

He looked up to where he could see Sedela's face peeping down at him.

Only somebody as slim and small as she was could have wedged herself between the roof and the boards.

"You are safe now," he said quietly, "and it was

clever of you to get up there."

"I . . . I am not . . . certain how I can . . . get down," Sedela whispered.

"I will catch you."

He moved so that her feet were above his head and she pushed herself backwards until she was hanging directly above him.

"Let yourself go now!" he ordered.

He thought she drew in her breath as if she were afraid.

Then she let herself go.

She was very light and she fell into the Marquis's arms.

He held her closely, taking only one step backwards to steady himself.

Sedela felt his arms around her, and knowing that she need no longer be afraid, she burst into tears.

"Oh . . . Ivan," she sobbed, "h-how could they . . . do that to me . . . and it was so . . . t-terrifying in the d-dark."

"I know," the Marquis said soothingly, "but it is all over now. The cobra is dead, and it is something that will never happen again."

"Th-they were . . . trying to . . . hurt . . . you!"

She looked up at him as she spoke.

He could see the tears glistening on her cheeks and the anxiety in her eyes.

He knew of no other woman who would think at this moment not of herself, but of him.

Without speaking, he bent his head and found her lips.

He felt Sedela stiffen in surprise.

But as his mouth took possession of hers, she

melted into him and they were no longer two people, but one.

To Sedela it was as if she had been taken from the darkness of Hell into the glory of Heaven.

She had been so certain until Ivan came that the snake would find some way of reaching her.

Then she would die ignominiously.

She would scream in terror, but no one would hear her.

Perhaps when she was dead no one would find her for days, if not weeks.

But when she heard Ivan's voice, she had known that God had heard her prayers.

In some miraculous way Ivan had come like the Archangel Michael to save her.

Even the few words they spoke, however, must have alerted the snake.

After Ivan left her, Sedela had heard the cobra slithering round the floor, then climbing onto the chair.

She thought it would somehow creep up the wall.

Then it would be twisting itself across the boards towards her.

But Ivan had come back.

He had killed the cobra and like a Knight in Shining Armour rescued her from death.

Her love seemed to rise within her like a great wave.

It was moving through her body into her breast and up to her lips.

She had never been kissed before.

Yet she knew that as Ivan kissed her and went on kissing her it was just how she imagined a kiss would be, only far, far more wonderful.

It was so perfect, so ecstatic, that she thought if she died now, she would have known this perfection of life.

Then she had no wish to die.

She wanted to live and for Ivan to kiss her and go on kissing her forever.

He raised his head.

Sedela could not help saying incoherently:

"I . . . I love you . . . oh, Ivan . . . I love you . . . I . . . love . . . you!"

The rapture in her voice was very moving, and the Marquis smiled before he kissed her again.

It was a long kiss and a very demanding one. He sounded breathless as he said:

"Come, my precious, let us get out of this place and go home."

It was then that Sedela felt as if she had come back to earth from the sky.

There was a little quiver in her voice as she asked:

"H-has . . . everybody . . . g-gone?"

"A long time ago," the Marquis replied. "It was Nanny who told me that you were missing."

"I thought . . . perhaps she would be the . . . only person who was . . . likely to be . . . aware that . . . something was . . . wrong."

"How could I have known—how could I have guessed," the Marquis asked, "that those devils could do anything so evil—so inhuman—to you, of all people!"

He was drawing Sedela out of the wooden house as he spoke.

Where she stood in the moonlight he thought

no one could be more lovely, more ethereal.

Their eyes met, and for a moment it was hard to think of anything except themselves.

Then the Marquis said quietly:

"It would be a mistake for anyone to know what happened here to-night. Are you brave enough to pretend that you hurt your ankle when you were in the garden? There was no one to help you until I found you and carried you back."

"Y-yes . . . of course," Sedela agreed. "You don't want to have people . . . talking about . . . the . . . snake."

"There will be nothing to prove that it was put there intentionally," the Marquis said, "unless you talk about what has happened."

"Of course, I . . . understand . . . that," Sedela agreed.

"It was Bayford, I suppose," the Marquis said in a hard voice.

Sedela nodded.

"I ought to call him out and teach him a lesson he will never forget!" the Marquis exclaimed.

"No . . . no . . . of course not!"

"But that would mean," the Marquis went on as if she had not spoken, "your name being involved and people discussing my affair with Esther Hasting even more than they are doing at the moment."

Sedela gave a little cry.

"That must not happen! We will . . . tell Nanny and . . . everybody else that I . . . hurt my . . . ankle."

As if she could not help herself, she moved a

little closer to the Marquis.

"Oh, Ivan . . . suppose . . . having failed to . . . kill me . . . they somehow . . . manage to . . . hurt or . . . destroy you?"

"They will not destroy me," the Marquis said harshly. "What they want is that I should marry Esther."

"Oh . . . Ivan!"

Without really meaning to, without thinking what she was doing, Sedela hid her face against his shoulder.

He knew she was struggling to prevent herself from crying again.

"I have the answer to that problem," he said, "but first I am going to take you home."

He picked up his pistol and put it into the pocket of his evening-coat.

Leaving the candle-lantern on the ground, he picked Sedela up in his arms.

"Now, remember which leg you are supposed to have injured," he said, "and let us hope I can climb down the path without dropping you!"

He was teasing her.

She managed to give a little laugh before she replied:

"I could . . . walk as far . . . as the house."

"If we are going to tell a lie," the Marquis said firmly, "we will tell a good one. One never knows if somebody might be looking out of a window, or a bird has forgotten to put his head under his wing."

Sedela put her head on his shoulder.

"I am quite . . . content for . . . you to carry . . . me," she said, "and I left my slippers . . . behind in the . . . wooden house."

"I will collect them to-morrow," the Marquis said, "and I will also bury the cobra's body."

He paused before he went on:

"I suppose really I should be extremely annoyed with the people from the Circus for selling it."

"I do not expect they had any idea what it was wanted for," Sedela answered, "and Lord Bayford had to pay a lot of money for it."

"How do you know that?" the Marquis asked.

"When he put the cloth over my head and carried me into the wooden house, I had, of course, no idea who he was," Sedela replied. "Then I listened and heard him being angry with the man who had fetched me away from the Fireworks by telling me there had been an accident."

"An accident!" the Marquis exclaimed.

"He had not brought the . . . snake as Lord Bayford had told him to do . . . from the Circus people," Sedela finished.

"It was a crafty idea," the Marquis said angrily, "but go on!"

"He then went himself to fetch it because his accomplice said they wanted a further twenty pounds for the cobra."

Sedela gave a little sigh.

"It was then when I was very frightened that I remembered how the arrow on the roof had caused the rain to leak into the house and that boards had been put up beneath it."

"I had forgotten that myself," the Marquis admitted, "until I saw you looking down at me. I can only thank God, my darling, that I was able to save you."

"I prayed that you would come."

"I heard your prayers," the Marquis answered.

"You did?" Sedela asked. "You did . . . really?"

"I thought you were calling me when I was going upstairs to make sure you were there and I found Nanny waiting for me."

"Oh, Ivan, it must have been when I was praying that you would somehow rescue me, though I could not believe it was . . . possible!"

"But it was possible," the Marquis said, "and it is something you must not think about again from this moment on."

Sedela raised her head from his shoulder.

They had reached the house.

The Marquis carried her in, along the corridor to his Study, and opened the door.

Still carrying her, he took her to the sofa and set her down.

Then he went back into the corridor to fetch one of the lighted candles.

From it he lit the candelabrum which stood on his desk.

Going to the grog-tray in a corner of the room, he poured out a drink for Sedela and one for himself.

"I think we both need this," he said. "If you were frightened, my darling, I knew as I ran back to the house to get my pistol that I have never, even during the Battle of Waterloo, been so terrified that I would not be in time."

"Oh, Ivan . . . that is a very . . . flattering thing to . . . say!"

The wine brought a little colour back into her cheeks.

Despite all she had been through, the Marquis thought no other woman could have looked so lovely and at the same time be so composed.

He knew that Esther or any of the other women he had pursued in London would be still screaming hysterically over their ordeal.

Instead of which, Sedela was just looking at him, her eyes filled with love.

The Marquis put down his glass and sat down beside her.

"You told me just now," he said in a deep voice, "that you wanted to save me from any more of these extremely unpleasant schemes on the part of Esther Hasting and Roger Bayford."

Sedela gave a little cry.

"Of course I want to do that! Oh, Ivan, suppose they . . . trap you in some . . . horrible way into making you . . . marry Lady Esther?"

She drew in her breath before she went on:

"They might . . . drug you when you are . . . least expecting it, or . . . force you . . . by threatening to . . . kill you, to make her . . . your wife!"

It was difficult for Sedela to say the last two words.

Then she was worried in case she had embarrassed the Marquis by what she had said.

Perhaps he would think she was being over-dramatic.

Once again she hid her face against his shoulder.

The Marquis put his arms around her and kissed her hair.

Then he said very softly:

"I have a solution which will keep me safe forever—that is, if you will agree to it."

"You have a solution?" Sedela repeated. "Oh, Ivan . . . what is it."

She raised her face to look up at him.

Once again he saw the anxiety in her eyes.

He could feel, too, that her body was trembling because she was afraid for him.

"As you know," the Marquis said slowly, "Esther Hasting is determined to marry me, but it would be impossible for her to do so or, as you suggest, to trap me into marriage, if I already have a wife."

Sedela stared at him.

He watched her and waited for her to understand what he was saying.

Then a dazzling light, as if it came from the stars, appeared in her eyes.

A faint glow of colour like the dawn of a new day suffused her cheeks.

She looked beautiful, radiant!

At the same time, because she was not quite certain what he was saying, her lips quivered a little.

He knew, too, that she was holding her breath as if it were impossible for her to breathe.

"We will be married in the Chapel as soon as possible after your parents return."

"Oh . . . Ivan . . . do you really . . . want me?"

It was the cry of a child who was suddenly afraid that something wonderful which had been promised would not materialise.

"I want you," the Marquis said, "more than it

is possible to tell you in words."

He bent his head and his lips took possession of hers.

He kissed her in what Sedela knew was now a different way.

He was telling her of his love.

It was the love that she had always dreamed of but could not hope she would ever find.

Once again she felt as if he carried her up into the glory of Heaven.

They were neither of them on earth, but a part of God.

They were already so close that nothing human could make them any closer.

"I love you, my precious darling!" the Marquis said, and his voice was deep and a little unsteady.

"I have loved you . . . ever since I can remember," Sedela murmured, "but . . . but I did not . . . know that what I . . . felt was the . . . love of a . . . woman for . . . a man."

"And now it is?" the Marquis asked.

"It is so . . . wonderful . . . so perfect . . . so holy . . . there are no words to . . . describe it!"

"We have all our lives to tell each other how much our love means," the Marquis said, "so now, my darling, I am going to send you to bed. You have been through a terrifying experience which is a secret we will never speak of again. I want you to think only of the future, when you will be my wife."

"How could I . . . think of . . . anything else except . . . you?" Sedela whispered.

The Marquis drew her to her feet.

Then, as if he could not help himself, he pulled her close.

He kissed her passionately and possessively and almost fiercely until they were both breathless.

"I want to go on kissing you all night," he said, "but that will have to wait until we are married. We must not forget that Nanny is waiting anxiously to know what has happened to you."

Sedela laughed.

"You have said the only thing that could make me leave you! I cannot let Nanny be worried."

"She is very worried," the Marquis answered. "She thought she saw Lady Constance and knew you were in danger."

"Lady Constance appeared . . . because of . . . me?" Sedela asked. "That makes me know I really am a . . . member of the . . . family!"

"I think Lady Constance must have been anticipating our marriage," the Marquis said. "From now on you are a very important member of the family, and of course we cannot have Nanny sitting for ever in the Nursery with nothing to do!"

Sedela gave a little choked laugh.

At the same time, she looked a little shy.

"Oh, Ivan," she said, "you are . . . going too fast into the future.

Impulsively Sedela threw her arms around his neck and kissed him.

Then, before he could hold her closer still, she twisted herself free and ran towards the door.

"I am going to see Nanny," she said, "but . . . darling . . . darling . . . darling Ivan . . . I love you!"

Then she was gone.

The Marquis heard her footsteps as she ran down the corridor towards the hall.

He was already thinking ahead that the House-keeper would know where to find the wedding-veil.

It had been used by three generations of Wind-lesham brides.

And later he would take out from the safe a tiara for Sedela to wear on the wedding-veil.

He then walked across the room to draw back the curtains and open the window.

The sky was filled with stars.

He once again was remembering his mother and how she had said that his Guardian Angel was among them and looking after him.

How was it possible after to-night to believe any thing else?

He had been saved by Sedela, who loved him, from marring a woman who would disgrace not only him, but also his family, a woman who was both evil and determined.

How could he not be eternally grateful that at the same time he found somebody who loved him for himself not because he was rich and a Marquis, but as a man.

It was what he had always wanted, what he had dreamt he would find one day.

He knew the love he had for Sedela was some-thing very different from the entirely physical infatuation that he had had for Esther.

He knew now that he was right to be ashamed of his lack of perception.

How could he have been bemused by a woman who was beautiful but utterly despicable?

He felt he would never be sufficiently grateful that he had, by a miracle, escaped, or, rather, he had been saved, just as he had been able to save Sedela.

"I will make her as happy as I am," he swore, "and together we will spread happiness for the rest of our lives to all those with whom we come in contact."

He thought it would be very wonderful when the Nurseries upstairs were filled with his sons and daughters.

They, too, would be protected not only by their Guardian Angels in the sky, but also by the ghost of Lady Constance.

She would warn them, just as she had warned many generations of Windles if there was danger.

'I have so much to be thankful for,' the Marquis thought humbly.

He shut the window and pulled back the curtains.

He walked slowly along the corridor and up the stairs to the Master Suite.

He thought as he did so that very soon he would be the happiest man in the world, when he could hold Sedela in his arms and teach her about love.

The love of a man and a woman!

While she would teach him about the Love of God.

ABOUT THE AUTHOR

Barbara Cartland, the world's most famous romantic novelist, who is also an historian, playwright, lecturer, political speaker and television personality, has now written over 542 books and sold over six hundred and twenty million copies all over the world.

She has also had many historical works published and has written four autobiographies as well as the biographies of her mother and that of her brother, Ronald Cartland, who was the first Member of Parliament to be killed in the last war. This book has a preface by Sir Winston Churchill and has just been republished with an introduction by Sir Arthur Bryant.

Love at the Helm, a novel written with the help and inspiration of the late Earl Mountbatten of Burma, Great Uncle of His Royal Highness The Prince of Wales, is being sold for the Mountbatten Memorial Trust.

She has broken the world record for the last sixteen years by writing an average of twenty-three books a year. In the *Guinness Book of*

Records she is listed as the world's top-selling author.

Miss Cartland in 1978 sang an Album of Love Songs with the Royal Philharmonic Orchestra.

In private life Barbara Cartland, who is a Dame of the Order of St. John of Jerusalem, Chairman of the St. John Council in Hertfordshire and Deputy President of the St. John Ambulance Brigade, has fought for better conditions and salaries for Midwives and Nurses.

She championed the cause for the Elderly in 1956 invoking a Government Enquiry into the "Housing Conditions of Old People.'

In 1962 she had the Law of England changed so that Local Authorities had to provide camps for their own Gypsies. This has meant that since then thousands and thousands of Gypsy children have been able to go to School, which they had never been able to do in the past, as their caravans were moved every twenty-four hours by the Police.

There are now fourteen camps in Hertfordshire and Barbara Cartland has her own Romany Gypsy Camp called Barbaraville by the Gypsies.

Her designs "Decorating with Love' are being sold all over the U.S.A. and the National Home Fashions League made her, in 1981, "Woman of Achievement.'

She is unique in that she was one and two in the Dalton list of Best Sellers, and one week had four books in the top twenty.

Barbara Cartland's book *Getting Older, Growing Younger* has been published in Great Britain and the U.S.A. and her fifth cookery book, *The*

Romance of Food, is now being used by the House of Commons.

In 1984 she received at Kennedy Airport America's Bishop Wright Air Industry Award for her contribution to the development of aviation. In 1931 she and two R.A.F. Officers thought of, and carried, the first aeroplane-towed glider airmail.

During the War she was Chief Lady Welfare Officer in Bedfordshire looking after 20,000 Service men and women. She thought of having a pool of Wedding Dresses at the War Office so a Service Bride could hire a gown for the day.

She bought 1,000 gowns without coupons for the A.T.S., the W.A.A.F.'s and the W.R.E.N.S. In 1945 Barbara Cartland received the Certificate of Merit from Eastern Command.

In 1964 Barbara Cartland founded the National Association for Health of which she is the President, as a front for all the Health Stores and for any product made as alternative medicine.

This is now a £65 million turnover a year, with one third going in export.

In January 1988 she received *La Médaille de Vermeil de la Ville de Paris*. This is the highest award to be given in France by the City of Paris. She has sold 25 million books in France.

In March 1988 Barbara Cartland was asked by the Indian Government to open their Health Resort outside Delhi. This is almost the largest Health Resort in the world.

Barbara Cartland was received with great enthusiasm by her fans, who feted her at a reception in the City, and she received the gift of an embossed plate from the Government.

Barbara Cartland was made a Dame of the Order of the British Empire in the 1991 New Year's Honours List.